I0452372

Memory
is
a place
where
we burn

A novel by
Izaak David Diggs

ISBN 978-1-7345428-5-1
Cover photography by Ike James
Cover design/composition by Faera Lane
Released 17 May, 2021 (P)

Part one:
Fire Road

ONE

We're all going to die out here!
A man had been yelling that in front of the Major Dollar. He didn't look homeless or crazy. No, his clothes were decent. A baby stroller was next to him. Was it his? If the yelling man lost his shit what would happen to that baby?
We're all going to die out here!
A few feet away another man gripped the strap of a dark green duffel bag. He was watching the yelling man, trying to figure out if he should check on the baby--
No. There is nothing you can do. If you stay out here you will die.

The man with the duffel walked into the Major Dollar. A balding man with a large mustache was going through his billfold and shaking his head. He was thin and smelled like mint and cheap laundry soap.
"Hey! Bag man!"
The girl at the register was pointing at a large sign behind her head: *PLEASE CHECK BAGS.* She didn't look angry, more bored or tired from the heat. The man with the duffel didn't want his bag out of his sight but the girl looked too apathetic to mess with stuff.

The clerk traded his bag for a plastic spoon with "9" scrawled on it in fading ink. He put the spoon in his pocket and looked out the window at the parking lot. Were there any *familiar* cars out there? The man was pretty sure there weren't but the heat had been fucking with his usual sharpness.

The Major Dollar smelled like plastic and failing deodorant and things spoiling in the walk-in coolers. The man checked his phone---a text was overdue, the text that would rescue him from the music coming through a blown speaker and the fretful mustache man shaking his head as he wandered the aisles.

How long did he have before there was a problem? Ten minutes? Five? Air conditioning was a precious commodity and he wasn't a customer, just a tourist looking for sanctuary. A guard turned down the aisle he occupied. She was over six feet tall and easily two hundred and fifty pounds. The cheap button down shirt the guard wore was too small and discolored with sweat. Over one breast was a sticker with "Security" written on it. The guard was carrying a heavy looking wooden pole. After a moment, the man realized it was a rod for hanging clothes on; the Major Dollar clearly did not have the budget for an armed guard. The woman with the closet rod didn't break eye contact as she closed the distance between them, getting close enough for him to see that her face was shiny with sweat; it had to be close to ninety in the Major Dollar.
"If you ain't buyin', you leavin'!"
He nodded and bent down to pick up an abandoned basket, brandishing it for good effect. The guard nodded and went off to harass other potential moochers of the Major Dollar's iffy air-conditioning. Even after a couple of minutes of adjustment the smell of things spoiling in the coolers was intense: Pints of milk. Frozen pizzas that would fit in a coffee cup ring. Eighth pounds of greenish beef. The guard had doubled back to make sure that the man was making use of the basket that had been held up. Understanding his role, he looked down at the merchandise on the closest shelf: A two ounce bottle of water. A half ounce bag of peanuts. A package with four Triscuits in it. He threw two bottles of water in the basket. It would probably come in handy.

Where was that text? His ride was ten minutes overdue. How long could he prowl the aisles of the Major Dollar before the guard with the stained shirt and closet rod kicked him out? What then? How long could he last outside? Where would he go? Was there any place safe for him, anywhere he wouldn't be tracked down?

If you ain't buyin', you leavin'.

The guard's voice the next aisle over. A mewling man's voice claimed that he was trying to choose between a pack of two mini-donuts or a bag with five pretzels in it. It had to be Fretful Mustache man; it certainly seemed the perfect voice for him. Knowing his own time was limited, the man pulled his phone out to make sure the volume was on.

"If you ain't buyin', you leavin'!"

Maybe that's all the guard could say, a mute that had been taught to utter five words. Perhaps Major Dollar had a training school for them: How to glower and brandish closet rods. Learning one phrase that fits every occasion.

The text came in. He took his basket up to the counter and bought his two bottles of water. Was there even two dollars remaining in his account? The transaction was approved.

"You need a bag for them?"

The clerk looked nervous. Major Dollar was so cheap they probably dressed down clerks for every bag they gave out. The man shook his head as he handed over the plastic spoon with "9" written on it. The clerk looked around at her feet and pulled up his duffell with some effort.

"It's heavy."

He took it from her without acknowledging her comment, stuck the bottles of water in a side pocket, and left the store. In the outer area where they kept the shopping carts it was over a hundred. Beyond the exterior doors---

The man prepared himself but it wasn't enough. Even after fifteen minutes of Major Dollar's iffy air-conditioning the late morning heat was stunning; it reminded him of sticking your head in an oven when making sure something is cooked. A silver crossover sort of car was parked in a handicapped space with the flashers on. Was that it? It looked small...and old. There were three people inside. Maybe it was for someone else---

The car honked. The man staggered twenty feet to the right rear door. There weren't any brand or model designations on the car but it looked like a Hyundai Santa Fe. The car honked again. He opened the right rear door as the text instructed and dropped in. The driver was holding her hand out for his phone. She had a hard face and blonde hair pulled back in a strict ponytail with a cap on top. Las Vegas Gamblers. Something about that made the man uncomfortable; he didn't want *gamble* to play a role in their journey. The driver handed the phone back. The fan was roaring beside her but it had to be in the eighties in the car. Not Major Dollar hot but not much better.

"Is there something wrong with the air conditioner?"

The driver didn't respond until they were backed out of the space.

"It's 132 degrees."

She put the car in drive. The engine revved but the car didn't move.

"Again?"

A man's voice behind him. The new passenger didn't look back, he was watching the woman behind the wheel shift from drive to neutral and then back to drive trying to get the transmission to work. After a few moments of shifting the gears did what they were supposed to do and the Hyundai lurched out of the Major Dollar parking lot with a puff of dark smoke.

TWO

Either the person in the front seat was really small or the seat was empty.

The man leaned forward for a peak; there was a box there. Neatly wrapped in brown paper, between one and two feet square.

"All the driver will tell you is that box paid for the primo seat."

A voice from the third row. Chubby face, somewhere in his late twenties, Mexican or maybe Guatemalan. Jorge. A previous text said there would be a driver and two other passengers: Jorge and Jane. It had also instructed him that, for the duration of the journey, he would answer to Joe. Joe nodded in response, Jorge went back to whatever he was doing on his phone. The car fell into silence. A series of surface streets eventually led to an onramp which would take them on the freeway west. Joe began to unconsciously knead the heavy fabric of his duffel; he didn't like the freeway and e-trucks that raced along it with impunity. The last time he had been on it...

He had been in a dying piece of shit car with five other people. That thing was wheezing and wobbling, struggling and smoking to even reach sixty. E-trucks were shooting by in the left lane silent as ghosts or wraiths. One had come rushing up from behind as one passed, blasting a horn that sounded like the laughter of the Devil. The driver had looked in the rear view mirror with an expression that didn't inspire confidence.

"Shit..."

And then Joe was at work a few days later with no memory between the truck closing in on them and being at his desk.

Shit...

The roar of the engine brought him back into the present. He shifted again in an attempt to get comfortable with the bag on his lap.

"Sorry I took all the room in the trunk with my chair."

Joe looked at the woman sitting next to him. She was Asian---Korean?---and muscular from the waist up with spindly legs--

The chair must be a wheelchair.

Joe had been so wrapped up in the struggling transmission that he hadn't noticed the person a foot to his left.

Missing things was a problem. Missing something important could end badly.

"Don't worry about it, I like my bag with me."

She looked from him to the bag and nodded before going back to whatever she had been doing on her phone. Joe put the palm of one hand on the door glass, it was hot. He looked up at the gauges and saw that the engine temperature was a bit above normal. Would that be a problem? He had heard it was close to 150 in the open desert.

"It's three hundred miles to the City," Jane rubbed her hands together. "What is that going to be, driver, four hours or so?"

"We might have to slow for the mountains so it could be five."

As she said that they passed an abandoned car; it looked a lot like the one they were riding in.

"Wonder what happened to those people?" Joe mused.

Jorge chuckled from the third row.

"That's a bad question to ask out here, buddy."

Joe already knew or believed he knew from what he had heard: If you broke down people probably wouldn't stop. They would worry about being jacked or at least having to share their water supplies. They would calculate the risk of taking on extra people into their already taxed car.

If you broke down you were on your own.

THREE

Driving at seventy, the driver kept them in the right lane. Every couple of minutes an automated e-truck would grow larger behind them and eventually shoot by in the left lane. Joe watched each one pass; they had to be going at least ninety.
Shit.
There had been a song on the radio, something really old. All he could remember was one line about the "year of the cat--"
And then he was back in his tiny cubicle processing invoices or whatever he had done at that temp gig. The tightness of bruises hidden by his clothes. A black eye. Memories his instincts begged him to question.

The box had a seat belt around it. Joe leaned forward to peak around the seat on the right side. The driver was watching him out of the corner of her eye. What would she do if he touched the box? If he undid the seatbelt to pick it up and shake it? Her eyes were hard and there was a dark gun like shape in the pocket molded onto her door. What would she do? He had experienced enough to have a few ideas and those ideas kept him from even tapping the box with a pinkie.
Joe sat back. The others had been watching himself.
"Maybe it's drugs," Jorge offered.
"Maybe it's a human head." Jane sighed.
"What do you think it is, driver?" Jorge asked.
The woman behind the wheel looked to the left so no one could see her expression in the rear view mirror.
"I think it's none of our business."
She had a harsh voice. Not stern, more like the tone of someone who spent years barking out orders to underlings or had been smoking before they had breasts. The voice had been around---
Do not fuck with me.
That's what the voice told Joe.

When they came upon slower traffic in the right lane, the driver would have to wait until the opportunity to pass without one of the automated semis bearing on them presented itself.

Shit.

"You keep looking in the rear view mirror." Jane, sounding uninterested while making an observation that was kind of like a question.

"E-trucks make me nervous is all," Joe explained.

"Yeah, me too." Jorge, his mouth full of something crunchy. "I've heard that they *can't* stop or maybe that they *won't* stop."

He shoved more food in his mouth and shook his head.

"They run you off the road, who the fuck are you gonna sue if you're dead?"

Joe understood that he was obsessing and tried to distract himself by focusing on the scenery: Dead earth with stunted shrubs. Rimrock in the distance. Heat mirages on the asphalt up ahead---

What would happen if one of those trucks traveling ninety rammed you from behind? Would you be obliterated or just bumped off the road? What then? He looked up at the small gauge on the dash registering outside temperature---it claimed that it was 140 outside. 140: If the car broke down how long could they survive out there? He thought of the two tiny water bottles in his bag before looking over his shoulder at the left lane again.

They had come upon an old SUV in the slow lane belching blue smoke. The driver crossed the line to pass.

"Oh, fuck."

Joe looked over his left shoulder at the lane behind them; a semi was approaching fast. He heard the motor in their car roar in an attempt to answer the driver's request for more speed. Seventy-five. Eighty. It seemed that the SUV belching smoke had somehow sped up.

And the temperature gauge was rising; it was now halfway between the median and three quarters.

They were almost past the old SUV when Joe thought he heard a new rattling noise from a few feet in front of him. What was that?

Something unimportant like a loose exhaust? Or, something more critical that could lead to them breaking down?

The approaching semi now filled the rear window. The driver cut to the right, barely clearing the SUV in the slow lane. The driver dropped them back down to seventy, her hands kneading the wheel.

The fretful hands said *I fucked up*.

She had miscalculated, she was fallible.

Their driver being fallible could get them killed.

FOUR

"Does this thing have bluetooth? I can hook up my playlists if it does." Jorge again.

"No music, I need to listen to the engine," the driver said.

I need to listen to the engine. Why? Did she know something the rest of them didn't? What was she hiding about her shitty car?

Joe pressed his palm against the window again, it was nearly too hot to touch. The original plan had been to take a night car---

That was the original plan until he realized that he had minutes and not hours to get out of town.

"Listen: When we get to the mountains I may need to turn the air conditioner off," the driver said firmly. "We may need to roll down the windows if the car starts overheating---"

"It's over 140," Joe pointed out.

"You can always get out and walk, pal."

"I'm just saying," the man with the duffel continued. "We paid you good money---"

"And I'll get you there; to do that I may need to kill the AC or maybe not. Worst case scenario."

The conversation was going nowhere. Joe focused on the passing scenery again.

"It should be cooler in the mountains," Jane said.

She was playing a game on her phone, Boomvest.

"Yeah, good point."

What was her story? The unspoken rule was not to ask. Also, Joe understood that if he asked for Jane's story he would have to tell his own.

That was an unspoken rule if you broke the first unspoken rule.

The rules didn't quell his curiosity about the three people he was sharing the car with---

The three people he would die with if the car broke down.

There was a smell in the car. Not Jorge's snacks, not sweat; something putrid that reminded him of the struggling coolers in the Major Dollar.

"What the fuck is that smell?" Jane. Good, it wasn't just him.

"It ain't me." Jorge, probably sensitive: *They always blame the fat guy for foul smells.*

Joe leaned forward towards the front seat.

"Seems to be stronger up here, maybe it's coming from the box."

The driver was getting annoyed by the conversation, frowning and shaking her head but saying nothing.

"Come on, driver, you *have* to be curious about what's in the box."

She said nothing in response. The car fell into a silence broken only by Jorge opening a new bag.

FIVE

Shit.

Had he seen any of the five people again? They had been casual acquaintances, sure, but Joe remembered all of them being in the same social circle.

Back in the easy days of fun friends and drinking.

Before whatever had happened on the freeway and he lost a few days.

"143. Shit, think this the hottest I've ever been in."

Jorge, leaning forward. He smelled like sour cream and onion potato chips. Joe glanced up at the engine temp; it hadn't dropped, if anything it had edged a bit closer to three-quarters of the way to boil over. How far were they from the city they had left if they had to turn back? Not that turning back was an option: There were few exits out there as there weren't any side roads or towns or even barns.

A hitch in the engine, a slight hiccup but enough for Joe to feel a wave of cold run through his body.

"You are...like radiating tension," Jane said.

There was a coldness to her voice--had struggling with her handicap made her hard? It was a rough enough world without having to get through it in a wheelchair.

"Sorry. It's been a rough few days and this isn't helping."

Rough few days, I really did just say that to someone who can't use their legs.

"Obviously it's been a rough few days for all of us or we wouldn't be in this shitty car trying to cross the desert in the middle of the day--no offense, driver."

A grunt from the woman behind the wheel.

"I don't give a shit, ain't my car."

"They give you a different car each trip?" Joe asked.

The driver didn't respond for long enough that Jane went back to her phone.

"No, I'm always in this car."

Jane stretched her arms out. Joe noticed her well developed triceps and the odor of sweat from her armpits---
What was that black stuff on her right hand? Dirt? Gunpowder?

Gunpowder? Are you fucking serious? Okay, well, at least you aren't obsessing about the engine rattle anymore...the one that has changed, sounds looser, almost a banging.

Jane quickly folded her hand into her lap. It seemed a furtive motion---had she caught him looking at her hand? Had she realized that Joe had seen the black residue? What if she knew that he knew it was gunpowder? Would he be a loose end to tie up at the end of the trip?

Okay...you have gone from stupid to completely fucking ridiculous...

SIX

The mountains were maybe ten miles ahead of them. And then what? Would the temp gauge climb even higher? What about that rattling? It definitely *was* getting louder.

"Either we're going to die or we aren't, worrying won't make it better or worse."

Joe looked over at Jane. He started rummaging through his mind for an apology that wouldn't sound like making excuses, especially to a woman who couldn't use---

"They're racing," the driver said. Her voice was softer than usual, almost as if she was talking to herself. "Didn't know they did that."

Her three passengers looked over their shoulders. Two e-trucks were approaching quickly from behind, neck in neck.

Yeah, it looked like they were racing...or working together to force the Hyundai off the road.

"Can we just pull off?"

"Look at that shoulder--see how it slopes? This thing is two wheel drive."

"What about the center median?"

"Again, too rough too pull out quickly; if we don't pull out quickly enough...you can guess the rest."

The trucks were gaining fast.

"I know of a good pull out maybe two miles ahead," the driver sighed. "Guess we'll have to risk speed."

Risk speed. Great. Joe began kneading his duffel again but said nothing. The engine roared even louder as the driver turned the air conditioner down one click then two. They passed eighty miles per hour.

The e-trucks were still gaining.

"I've heard those trucks can go a hundred." Jorge, not helping.

Joe focused on the headrest in front of him or tried to--

Nope, had to glance at the speedometer again. Eighty-five.

The trucks were still gaining and the Hyundai was starting to wobble.

The temp gauge had crept up even with air on a lower setting, it was now at the three-quarters mark.

Ninety miles per hour. If they had a blowout at that speed---

Why are you even going there?

For the first time Joe noticed the odometer was closing on 250,000 miles.

Had the tie-rods ever been replaced?

The trucks were still neck and neck; they were less than a quarter mile behind the Hyundai and closing the distance.

"This could be a little rough."

The driver hit the brakes and bounced onto a large turnout as the trucks shot past.

The horns blasting almost sounded like laughter.

The driver slewed back onto the freeway once the trucks were clear, barely having enough turnout. She got them back up to seventy and studied the gauges.

"Hey, driver, now that we're not racing can we get the air back on high?"

"Can you see the temp gauge? We're not even climbing yet. I have to get the temp down before we hit those mountains."

144. Was this a record? No, they had been recording temperatures of as high as 160 in other parts of the world.

SEVEN

Two ravens were circling off to the north: Didn't they need to shelter when it was so hot? Even in the car it was hotter than it had been in the Major Dollar. Joe contemplated his bottles of water: What if he pulled one out? Would he be obligated to offer the other one to Jorge or Jane? What about the driver? As he fretted, the driver reached down in the front passenger footwell and grabbed a large bottle of water. Joe marvelled at what had to be a 48 ouncer; that was a serious bottle of water.

She is prepared...prepared for when this car takes a shit and leaves us on the side of the road. And that dark shape in the door has to be a gun; insurance that we won't fiddle with that box or make a grab for that majestic bottle of water.

He had seen a kid stabbing another child over a bottle of water like that. Both had been eight---

"What are you daydreaming about over there?"

"Hey, you know the rules, Jane---"

"It's okay, driver. It's a story I wrote a couple of years ago: It was a hot day like this, one eight year old stabbed another over a bottle of water."

It had happened from only a few feet away from where he had been standing. The stabbed child hadn't cried out, just grunted and doubled over. The kid with the knife easily took the water bottle and walked away. She didn't run, it was too hot for running. The injured child had sunk into a sitting position. There were people around but they weren't seeing or sensing anything aside from the heat at the bus stop they were all waiting at. The memory was nearly bringing Joe to tears, the others in the car seemed blase.

"Shitty story." Jane, moving her left hand to crack her right wrist over and over. "Kid die?"

"I don't know. I called an ambulance but the kid didn't want it. *Gotta go home or I'll be in trouble.* He was stabbed and was worried about being in trouble. I told him he was being silly. He told me to mind my own fucking business; a little kid said that to me."

17

"Little kid who got shanked." Jane, now cracking her left wrist.
"You gotta be tough to hang out at bus stops these days."

Oh my God, poor little guy!
How terrible! Oh--what a cruel world we live in!
The stabbing story usually got those sorts of responses. Not from the
other people in the Hyundai: *You gotta be tough to hang out at bus
stops these days,* that's what the story got from Jane. Even Jorge,
who seemed like an easy going friendly guy, was back to his snacks
and phone.
*If this car breaks down these are the people I will share that
situation with. There will be no banding together, it will be Lord of
the fucking Flies time.*
The temp gauge had eased down some but was still between the
mid-mark and three quarters as they began climbing. The driver let
their speed drop some. With the air conditioner on half it was hot
enough that Joe began to swoon. He looked out his window so the
others couldn't see.
Like I'm gonna show any weakness to this lot.

EIGHT

The outside air was now 135. Maybe it would drop as low as 120 up the mountain, maybe even 110--still fucking hot.

I may need to shut the air conditioner off.

Honestly, rolling the windows down may have been an improvement. The heat and stuffiness of the car was reminding Joe why he didn't like saunas: Breathing in hot. The constant flow of sweat. The body odor of strangers. Joe thought that he had become immune to the stink of overheated bodies, clearly he had been wrong---it was like breathing through a dirty sock that had been sitting in an oven.

"I wonder what happened to that kid..." Jorge, his voice soft, contemplative.

"The one who got stabbed?"

"Nah, the stabber. What even happened to that girl? It was a girl, right?"

"Yeah. I don't know."

How was he comfortable back there? It looked like there wouldn't be much legroom.

Maybe he doesn't have legs. Maybe I died in that crash and I'm on an endless trip through Purgatory--

Yeah, this sort of thinking is definitely not helping my anxiety.

"So...you a writer or something?"

"I guess. Journalist...not that that sort of writing exists anymore. Reporters."

He looked back at Jorge. The man in the far back looked confused but trying to be amiable. Joe plowed on, wishing he hadn't opened his mouth.

"I did some blogging and through that I got a job with this online journal that did local news."

And that was where all the problems started: Writing about things he should have understood a lot of people wouldn't want written about--not that he was going to get into that with the others in the car.

The engine sounded different. It was working harder as they climbed into the mountains sure, but there was something else, something Joe couldn't place but instinctively realized was *bad*. The engine temp was now firmly at three-quarters to hot...

And then it was creeping past.

"Okay, guys, I have to shut the air conditioner down; roll your windows down."

Joe's window shuddered as it retracted into the door. Watching it, he struggled with his anger: How dare they use such a shitty car. He kept his feelings to himself understanding that venting wouldn't do any good. The temp gauge immediately dropped below three-quarters, not a lot but enough for the passengers to feel relief. It was still 125 degrees out, even with the air circulating at sixty miles per hour it was uncomfortable; the worst part was breathing the heat in.

"It feels like my lungs are being cooked." Jorge, his voice between a gasp and a moan.

Jane said nothing but Joe could see she was struggling with it. The driver took off her cap for a moment to mop some sweat off her forehead. There were grey streaks in her hair. How old was she? Her face looked early forties but clearly whatever years she'd lived had been tough ones. They were approaching an old RV fast. The camper had a big fluffy tail of blue smoke.

"That's going to be a treat to breathe." Jane, starting to crack her wrists again.

The driver let the Hyundai drop to fifty then forty-five to slow the approach as she studied her mirrors, looking for an e-truck approaching.

"The e-trucks slow during mountains, right?" Joe asked.

"Not really," Jorge said. "The only problem they have is their batteries drain more quickly going up the mountains. I read that they regain it through kinetic energy when braking on downslopes."

You are not just a fat idiot who won't stop snacking.

Joe's was thinking that as they entered the blue smoke. Even though it had dissipated some it still made all four of them cough. You could taste it, the toxic flavor of weeks or even months being taken off your life.

"Okay, I think we're clear; I'm going around."

The driver got in the left lane and pushed the Hyundai back up to speed. The roar of the engine sounded desperate, on the verge of something snapping or exploding. Joe knew not to look at the speed or the temp or the rear view mirror. Instead, he focused on the rough canyons they were passing through carved out of red rocks.

"This really is a beautiful place..." Jorge, almost a sigh.

It was. If only they were passing through it under different circumstances.

"You sure? All I see is blue fucking smoke." Jane rasped, her breathing labored.

As they went around the RV the blue smoke was so thick they could barely see each other. Joe felt himself unable to breathe and knew he wasn't alone---what if the driver passed out?

We are all going to choke to death on this smoke, we can't---

And then the driver was pulling in front of the old camper and the smoke was being sucked out of the Hyundai.

"Well...that was incredibly unpleasant," Joe said.

"You still think this is a beautiful place?" Jane turned to ask Jorge.

"Under different circumstances," the man in the back replied meekly.

"I can't believe people worked on a road around here, can you imagine how fucking hot that would have been?" Jane mused.

"It wasn't nearly as hot back then," Jorge replied

"Still would have been hot doing road work." Jane, cracking her knuckles.

"Shit..."

The driver. All three of her passengers looked up at the temp gauge--passing the RV and pushing the engine had taken it between three-quarters and boil over.

"I think that's the pass up ahead," Joe offered.

"It better be or we're completely fucked," Jane said flatly.

An e-truck was approaching in the left lane. It wasn't doing ninety as it would have been on the flats but even the seventy or so it managed was impressive.

At the summit the temperature was 108.

"It's weird how 108 can feel almost cool and refreshing," Joe said.

"Yeah, I was thinking the same thing," Jorge smiled.

NINE

The outside air temperature quickly began climbing when they began their descent: 108. 115. 120---

The struggle over, the engine stopped moving towards boil over and dropped below three-quarters again.

"We're in the clear. I'm going to turn on the air conditioner again. Give it a minute, though, before rolling your windows up."

The driver had turned it on full.

"Awesome, I was hoping you'd put it on full blast," Jorge laughed gently.

"Get out of my head; this is like luxury or something," Joe smiled himself.

"Oh...you've *got* to fucking be kidding me," he added with a whine.

"What?" The driver asked.

"My window, it's not rolling up."

"Your button may be broke; stop pushing it, let me try from up here."

Nothing happened aside from what smelled like burning plastic inside Joe's door.

"Hey...something is overheating, we gotta stop trying to roll it up."

"Driver--what is up with this shitty car? This is no joke, it'll probably be 140 again when we reach the flats!"

"Hey, don't yell at me, I'm stuck right here with you guys. This ain't my car, I just drive it."

"Everyone chill, we can use the plastic bag my food was in to cover the window---"

"I got some duct tape in my bag."

Jane, Joe found himself looking at her hand again.

Yeah, that black stuff definitely looks like a powder burn.

Jorge and Jane handed over the window fixing supplies. Joe began struggling to tape the bags to the window frame, the wind nearly sucking a bag out.

"You might want to tape those bags together first," Jane pointed out.

"This would be a lot easier if we just pulled off for a minute..."

"Can't do that," the driver grunted.

"You worried about the RV and the blue smoke?" Jorge asked. "It probably won't be smoking as much on this downgrade."

The driver didn't speak for a minute. Watching her face in the rear view mirror, Joe could see she was sitting on some information that she didn't want to share.

"We can't stop all the way. The transmission has been acting weird, has difficulty engaging sometimes---"

Joe thought of the parking lot, had hoped it was the *beginning* of a problem, not one that had been *pre-existing*.

"Are you fucking serious?"

"Hey, it ain't my car, don't put this shit on me!"

"We shouldn't have left the city; if the transmission takes a shit out here we will die. Fuck, what were you thinking?"

"Okay, everyone just calm down." Jane motioned to Joe for the plastic bags. "Hand those bags over, I'll patch them together and then I will tape them up; I have some experience with this sort of thing."

She quickly made a sort of plastic quilt, deftly cutting the duct tape with her teeth, not a single wasted movement.

"Okay, now I need you to hoist me onto your lap."

A pause and her already quiet voice became even quieter.

"And If you get a boner I will fucking kill you."

Joe leaned over and grabbed her, feeling awkward about his hands on her buttocks. Jane was heavier than she looked, not fat but muscled. She was also hot, feverish hot; the warmth of another human being so close was almost unbearable. Luckily she worked fast and quickly had the makeshift window up in less than two minutes.

TEN

"We aren't square."

Jane, she sounded troubled by something.

"What do you mean?" Joe asked.

"You told us something about yourself, none of us have done that."

"That's okay---"

"No, it isn't. In situations like this you can't have debts with the people you're sharing that situation with."

She looked out the window. They were dropping down to a desert valley that had to be fifty miles across, endless baked earth with tiny scrub brushes here and there.

"I see everything, see you looking."

"What do you mean?" Joe said that knowing what she meant.

"You're looking at the black stuff on my hand."

"I didn't mean anything by it."

"I'm not accusing you, I'm just saying I noticed."

Jane paused, looked down at her legs. What did she see when she looked at them? Had she been born without use of them or had there been an accident? She seemed military in bearing---maybe she had been in the War and gotten shot or perhaps her team had driven over a landmine or something.

"It is what you think it is, that's all I want to say. I feel that will pay off the debt."

"How do you know what I think it is?"

She looked Joe directly in the eye---

Yeah, they both knew what the black mark was.

The downgrade grew steeper. Each time the driver pumped the brake the car made a groaning sound and a burning smell started coming through the vents. Brakes.

The brakes are burning up. If the driver doesn't allow more freewheel, they will probably catch on fire. On the other hand, how fast can we go before she loses control?

Their speed rose from sixty to seventy and then seventy-five. The plastic window billowed and pushed at the tape. The duct tape resisted but gaps were forming creating air whistles. The driver had to keep pumping the brakes or risk losing control on the curves. "Jorge, would you please get as far to the right on your seat? Jane, would you mind getting on Joe's lap again?"

"You think I wanna be without a seatbelt during this shit?"

"If I lose control seatbelts won't save you---what the fuck?"

"What?"

"You're not going to believe this…"

The RV was coming up fast behind them.

"Jesus--get in the left lane! Let them get by!"

"No, they plan to pass, I've been watching them; they have to do it very gradually or they'll lose control."

"They have to be going well over eighty."

"Yeah, they must have lost their brakes."

The RV was only a few hundred feet behind and struggling to get in the left lane without losing control. The driver eased as far to the right as she dared and the old camper shot past. It attempted to make the curve only to go up on three wheels. The driver of the RV attempted to get all six wheels back on the asphalt by turning to the left but the correction was too much and the old camper burst through the guardrail and shot over the edge.

"Holy shit!"

"Yeah, now it's our turn."

Jane was on his lap now but Joe didn't notice. All he felt was the old Hyundai leaning to the left, the tires chirping and then squealing in protest. It didn't feel right, felt like the car was breaking from the arc they'd been taking on the inside of the curve.

We're going to die, maybe we'll land on top of the burning R.V.

"Oh, shit." The driver, more of a sigh than anything.

Joe closed his eyes. There had been a girl on his lap in the other piece of crap car; another detail coming back: She was a sunny blonde and he had clumsily flirted with her. The blonde had flirted back but she had been flirting with everyone---yeah, he was remembering that as well. Had she been the last one in the car? Yes, with no place else to sit the blonde had sat on Joe's lap. He had laughed and played it off but inside he had been thrilled, the chance to be close to someone he found attractive after many days and nights in his room in his world alone. Up close, the girl smelled like sweat, maybe a bit unclean. Joe could smell alcohol coming through her pores, smell a cloying perfume---

Oh, shit.

And then he had been sitting in that cubicle, feeling aches and bruises.

And a few days after that, attempting to gather information from friends and coming up with nothing. Had it been a false memory? How could a false memory be so vivid right down to the feel of the fabric of the blonde's summer dress on his face? The sight of a black bra strap as the shoulder of her dress shifted.

Joe felt rough hands on his, guiding them; Jane putting his hands over her breasts as they braced for going through the guardrail. They were firm and her nipples felt hard. He didn't open his eyes; it would be bad enough to *feel* the crash, he didn't want to *see* it.

Despite every indication the driver maintained control. They would live. Joe dropped his hands from Jane's breasts. The car was silent again.

"Could you help me back into my seat?"

He did, careful to be respectful how he handled her, wondering why she had done that with his hands. Jane buckled back up and looked out her window. Joe looked over at her, realized there was nothing to say, and looked out his own window.

ELEVEN

They reached the valley. The driver got the old Hyundai back up to seventy and the temp gauge steadied halfway between the mid-range and three-quarters. Off to their left, the RV was mangled and ablaze. Had the people died on impact? Had they survived the impact---broken but somehow alive---only to perish in fire and smoke?

"That fire is really big."

"It *was* an R.V.; they probably had propane tanks or something."

"I wonder what they were thinking when they went over…"

"It probably wasn't a coherent thought." The driver, a new expression on her face---*sadness*. "Just panic and a fear too raw to put into words."

Jorge seemed to be the most entranced by the burning R.V.

"That R.V. was a piece of shit; those folks probably had a hard life." He opened the bag on another snack before continuing.

"I don't know...was it unfair that another shitty thing happened to them or was it a relief all the hardship ended?"

No one had an answer to that.

"I wonder about that girl, too," Jorge continued. "You know, the one who stabbed the boy for the bottle of water. Did she end up some fucked up sociopath, doing worse and worse things, or does it haunt her? How long ago did that happen, Joe?"

"Three years ago."

"She's eleven now, still a child---what will it be like when she's an adult? Who will she be? You have to wonder."

The car fell into silence. There was a boom in the distance, maybe a propane tank on the R.V. Joe looked over at the burning camper growing smaller at over a mile a minute.

Shit.

Some old song about a horse with no name had been on the stereo. The song was going into the chorus as the blonde on his lap was talking about some new food cart and then he was sitting in his cubicle entering something about inventories into a computer.

Five days later.

Was it really five days or had he just created that detail at some point? He had cuts and bruises and a bandage on his head to go with the memory of the moments leading up to a crash but---

Had there really been a crash? Even as the details grew in number and intensity he still wasn't sure.

TWELVE

The burning R.V. became a small orange dot in the distance; flickering, indistinct. The end of the valley up ahead was a new cause for concern.

"Looks like we're going to have to go over another pass," Jorge said.

"Yeah, but it's nothing like the last one; probably won't even need to turn off the AC," the driver said quietly.

"All the shit we've been through makes me think about the pioneers."

Jorge, looking down as he moved a zipper back and forth---a bag? His pants? Joe felt he had a good idea about the backgrounds of Jane and the driver; Jorge was a complete unknown.

"As bad as this has been, the pioneers probably had it way worse." Joe said.

Jorge grunted. A mile passed followed by another.

"Does anyone else smell baking bread?"

"Good, it isn't just me---"

"It reminds me of freshly baked croissants."

"It's not coming from back here, I think it's coming from the box."

"You guys are nuts." The driver, shaking her head as she concealed her expression from anyone watching the rear view mirror.

"You don't smell it, driver?"

There was no response to that. Joe and Jorge exchanged a look: *That's probably because she knows what's in the box.*

Jane gave both of them a sharp look: *Don't push it, we're depending on her to get us to the City.*

The smell of baked goods was too distinct to ignore, overpowering the smells of hot skin, sweat, and dirty clothes.

What smells like rot and then freshly baked bread an hour later? Both Jorge and Joe were thinking that; both knew not to voice their thoughts.

"We should be at about the halfway point."

Jane, she hadn't looked up from her phone---aside from the warning glance---since coming down the mountain.

"Yeah, maybe two hours until we get to the City," Jorge said.

They hadn't seen any other cars since the R.V. had shot over the edge, just e-trucks shooting past them silently in the fast lane or going in the opposite direction.

All the shit we've been through makes me think about the pioneers. Joe looked out at the valley they were crossing. What *had* it been like a hundred-fifty years earlier? Yeah, it hadn't been as hot, not even close, but instead of four hours it would have taken *weeks*. Was there any water out there? It sure didn't look like it. He was leaning forward to look out the front passenger window; it made his back ache. Joe watched the scenery partly out of interest, partly out of boredom, and partly to keep from looking at Jane. What had she meant by putting his hands on her breasts? He was slipping into fantasies of fucking her despite understanding it was the wrong time and place to have such thoughts.

THIRTEEN

"Who was the first one to be picked up?" That felt like a harmless question to Joe, a way to pass the time.

"You know the rules, Joe." The driver, looking in the mirror and shaking her head. She had a scar on her face, probably had sweated off the make-up she used to cover it.

"Me, though the box was already in the front seat."

Joe looked back at Jorge. The man in the back seat was wearing glasses as he worked on something. Feeling Joe's attention he looked up with a smile before going back to what he was working on.

"I'm tracking the rising of temperatures over the past twenty years," he offered. "Sort of blending that data with the flow of the Colorado over the same time period."

"Not much," Jane, under her breath.

"Yeah, Phoenix and Las Vegas are definitely cities that had no business growing the way they did."

"Are you some kind of scientist or something? Or a professor?"

Joe waited for the driver to chide him but she remained silent. Jorge looked up from his work and removed his glasses. He met Joe's gaze with a smile but there was wariness in his eyes.

"Something like that."

The driver muttered something and shut the AC down to half power. Joe leaned forward and saw the temp gauge was back to three-quarters and inching up. According to the readout on the middle of the dash, the outside air was 138 degrees.

"Remember when a hot day was 115?" Jorge laughed at that but his laughter was uneasy around the edges.

"I grew up in Portland, bro, we'd have maybe three or four days over *100*."

"Wow."

"Yeah, this year I read that *Alaska* had a full week over 100 degrees."

With the AC fan lower Joe could make out that the rattling sound was more distinct and it felt like the engine was missing a little, like one cylinder wasn't firing every few cycles or something. Unable to resist anymore, he pulled out one of his small bottles of water and took a drink, killing half of it with one sip. Jane looked over at him.

"I've got another one if you need water."

"I got water. You shouldn't offer your water, worry about yourself."

"I just thought, since we're in this situation together---"

"This situation doesn't change shit. You gotta look out for number one or you're gonna get fucked."

Was she being normal Harsh Jane or was it because of what had happened coming down the mountain? It was obvious to him that she had no interest in him, her voice and posture made that clear to Joe---

Her nipples had been hard; her bra had padding but he had been able to feel them---

Why was he obsessing about stupid shit like that? Joe faced forward and killed the bottle.

"Where did you even find a tiny ass bottle like that?"

"Major Dollar. I had to buy something or they would have kicked me out."

"Do they still have those pizzas the size of an ashtray?" Jorge asked.

"Yeah, I think I saw those."

The car fell into a silence broken only by the fluttering of the plastic in the window, the sound of the tires, and the occasional miss of the engine. Turning the AC down had stopped the engine temp from rising but it was holding at three-quarters. The heat was making Joe drowsy and he caught himself nodding off only to wake with a start a few seconds or minutes later.

Oh...shit!

The memory of the party car seemed so real but was it? None of his friends remembered his leaving with other people: *No, bro, you left by yourself. You were drunk, really drunk; I was worried about you getting home. Blonde girl in a light dress? Nope, you must have imagined that.*

But he could hear the laughter of the others, smell the hair of a girl that had ended up in his lap, see how the visible bra strap was fraying---
And then he was sitting in his cubicle.
And five days had passed.

FOURTEEN

"When we get to the City, I'm gonna go to the beach and just walk out into the ocean." Jorge, he sounded happy, almost like a child. Joe imagined the beaches as impossibly crowded with people desperate to escape the heat but knew to keep that to himself.
"The ocean would be great right now," he agreed.
"Then let's do it, unless you have something else going on."
"No. That---"
Joe was interrupted by an explosion and the car slewing.
"Fuck me," the driver, struggling to keep the car under control. There was a pullout up ahead, she steered the Hyundai into it and brought the car to a stop. The driver gripped the steering wheel and rested her head on it; her posture one of defeat. She looked down at the shifter, muttered something no one else could make out, and put it in park. The car was silent---was there a spare tire? Who was going to change it when it was 136 degrees outside? The driver started to unbuckle her seatbelt.
"No: If you pass out you can't drive. I should change the tire."
The driver looked back at Joe suspiciously.
How can you look at me like that? I'm risking myself to save all of us and you look at me like I'm gonna steal your wallet.
Anger and then realization:
She probably watched what I did to Jane in the rear view mirror and thought I groped her, maybe she didn't see that it was Jane putting her hands on me. Maybe the driver was raped and saw what I did as some rapist shit.
"Okay, yeah, thanks. Uh, there should be a jack and a lug wrench in the way back, you'll have to move Jane's chair out. The tire is under the body, I'll have to help you lower that."
The driver unlocked the doors but kept the motor running. The heat hit both of them; after over an hour of air conditioning it was unreal and brutal. Joe walked to the back and opened the hatch, pulling the wheelchair out and setting it gently behind the Hyundai. He was already sweating; his eyebrows were quickly overwhelmed and

sweat dripped into his eyes. The heat went through his nose and mouth and burned all the way down to his lungs where it simmered like embers.

"Oh...this just *sucks*."

He found the tools and closed the hatch, the driver took two pieces of metal, stuck them in a hole, and lowered the tire.

"Just leave the blown tire. It's too hot to fuck with trying to reattach it and winding the chain back up."

"Okay."

The driver put the chair back in and closed the hatch. Joe went to the dead tire to loosen the bolts. Just breathing the air made it feel like every drop of moisture inside him was evaporating and the little that was left had turned into the sweat that was blinding him. He tried to wipe it away with a forearm but that too had become covered in sweat.

I could fucking die out here changing a tire---what does heat stroke feel like?

Two more ravens circled overhead---

They're just waiting for me to drop and then down they'll come.

He loosened the lug nuts and found the jack point. The heat from the asphalt was coming through his shoes; the soles seemed to be getting softer, melting. Joe struggled to keep a grip on the lug wrench with his sweaty hands. When he misjudged through his blurred vision and dropped it his palms were too moist to retrieve it from the pavement. Fighting dizziness, he wiped his palms on his shorts and positioned the jack---

I will not puke, I will not puke, I can get through this...

Every breath was a burning ache he raised the car and wrestled the tire off---

And then he crumpled. Was he about to throw up the water he had just drank? The chances were good. Joe struggled back to his feet and staggered to where the spare lay. He heard the back door open and then felt a hand on his shoulder.

"Get back in the car, I got this from here."

Jorge, he did have legs after all. Joe nodded in thanks and climbed back into his seat. Jane pressed a bottle of water into his hands. "Drink this slow or you will definitely puke it up and I will fucking kill you for wasting water."

If the heat had done this to him what was it doing to Jorge? Joe couldn't do more than lay slumped in his seat, sipping on the bottle. A minute or a few minutes later, Jorge was opening the door. Joe climbed out so the other passenger could climb back into the third seat. The replacement tire was on and everyone was back in the car with the doors closed---why were they just sitting there?

The transmission.

Joe remembered how the driver had struggled to get it engaged in the parking lot; judging by the silence in the car everyone else was probably having the same recollection. The driver looked back at each of them in turn and then faced forward. Her hand went to the shifter and dropped it into drive:

The engine revved but the car didn't move. The only sound was the anger of the motor and then the rasp of it at idle.

The driver shifted back into park and put her hands on the wheel.

She seemed to be watching something over the car; maybe she saw the ravens, too.

"Don't be pissed at me---I'm stuck in this car with the rest of you."

Those words gently, more gently than you would think someone with such a hard face could speak.

She took a hand off the steering wheel and shifted into drive.

The driver took her foot off the brake, there was a moment that felt like five days and then the car lurched forward.

Joe and Jorge cheered, they couldn't help it; even Jane smiled.

The old Hyundai pulled back on the highway and slowly gained speed.

FIFTEEN

The valley ended and the highway began climbing. Unlike the last pass this one came promptly and with little effort. The descent was mild, as well.

"I was hoping we'd see the other city as we crested," Jorge said

"Nope, it's still a couple hours away," the driver replied.

Joe leaned forward to look at the gauges: Engine temp between half and three-quarters. Outside temp at 141. Was that an old cabin off a couple of miles to the north? It looked like it. An e-truck approached from behind them and shot past.

"Shit."

"What are you stressing about, driver? That truck didn't honk or anything."

"CBP."

"CBP?"

"Citizen's Border Patrol." Jane said, twisting to see what was behind them. "Vigilantes---"

"Yeah, now I know what you're talking about."

A newer truck with a bull bar and lift closed on them. Red lights mounted in the grill began flashing. Joe turned around to watch it approach. Even if they wanted to stop there was the matter of the transmission---what would the driver do? There was no way they could outrun that truck in the shitty Hyundai.

A passenger side window was opening on the truck, an arm in a khaki shirtsleeve was gesturing with a shotgun. The truck went into the passing lane.

"Hyundai driver, pull off to the side of the road now!"

Jane was doing something on her phone. To Joe it seemed a hell of a time to be playing Boomvest. The truck was now alongside them. It was lifted enough so that Joe couldn't see the shotgun or what the passenger looked like. In the front seat of the Hyundai, the driver looked over at the box and then rolled her window down. What was she going to do? Pull the gun he assumed she had and try to shoot a tire out? Shoot the man with the shotgun? CBP had to have more trucks with lights in the grill, more men with shotguns to lean out of windows.

And...why did she look at the Box before rolling her window down?

"I can't stop, the transmission is broke!" The driver yelled into the wind.

"We need to check your IDs," the passenger in the truck yelled over the wind.

"If we stop we might not be able to get going again!"

"This isn't optional!"

There was no point in pointing out to the men in the truck that they didn't have the authority to pull people over; they had multiple guns and a more powerful vehicle, they could do whatever they wanted. Joe thought of the security guard with the closet rod and the sticker on her blouse glowering at him. The driver was gripping the wheel with both hands. Joe could see in the rear view mirror that she was thinking and that she was worried.

If the driver is worried that means we are probably fucked.

"Hyundai driver, this is your one and only warning!" A different voice over the truck's P.A., not the passenger who had rolled down his window.

"Hey, if we got rolling before, we can probably get rolling again." Jorge, though it was clear by the tone of his voice he didn't want to stop.

"We're not fucking stopping." The driver, almost too soft to hear.

Jane had looked up from her phone and was looking straight ahead. The CBP truck passed and dropped into the lane in front of them.

Next come the brake lights. If we try and pass they will simply force us off the road.

No, the truck was gaining speed, quickly growing smaller.

"That makes no sense; their logical next move would have been to force us off the road; the CBP is notorious for that."the driver sounded confused.

And then Joe thought of how the truck had taken off shortly after Jane had finished typing something. He looked over at her. She looked back and shook her head. They both faced forward again.

39

"Wish we had a truck like that," the passenger in the third seat said. The driver looked back at Jorge.

"Hey, just sayin'," he added. "Think of how quickly we could get to the next city..."

SIXTEEN

Oh, shit…

And then what? The blonde had leaned against him---was she twisting to see what the driver saw?

And then Joe was sitting in a cubicle with healing bruises under his clothes.

He looked over at Jane---who had she been texting?

Maybe she killed someone for those people and they owed her.

Maybe she blew away someone causing trouble for them…

Joe didn't like those thoughts, didn't want to think of the ugliness of anyone in that car, not after what they'd been through with the blowout.

"You always seem to be thinking, Joe."

He looked over at Jane and gave her a meaningful look. She looked back, her expression neutral.

"Jorge and I are on our phones, the driver is driving, and you're looking out the window a lot or seem lost in your thoughts."

"I'm just glad that CBP truck didn't force us off the road."

Jane smiled a little and looked straight ahead again.

"Maybe they recognized the driver. Maybe she works for people they know."

The woman to his left stretched her arms and looked out her window.

"What story are you working on now?"

Joe waited for the driver to pipe up about "the rules." She remained silent; he was on his own.

"One there is no point in writing because my editor killed it."

Jane looked over at him expectantly; Joe could feel Jorge's attention…even the driver was watching him in the rear view mirror.

"They saw it as too risky to publish…"

The others were waiting for him to continue, maybe even the Box was listening.

"There was a scientist, rumor is that he found a cure for cancer…an easy cure, plants, nothing to do with big pharma. Someone began killing people around him. Supposedly he stopped his research and went into hiding."

Jane and the driver were still watching him. Jorge? Joe turned back to look at the man in the third seat. Jorge was looking down but not doing something on his phone.

"Are you some kind of scientist or something? Or a professor?"

"Something like that."

Joe faced forward again.

They were approaching a converted school bus painted a dozen different wild colors in patterns that seemed unrelated to one another.

"Bus people," Joe said quietly.

"Bus people?" Jane, not looking up from her game.

"You know, people who just live on old school buses, drifting around."

"I thought it had gotten too hot for that sort of shit."

The driver studied her mirrors, got in the left lane, and floored the pedal. The engine roared and the transmission kicked down. They got up to seventy-five and easily passed the bus. The driver smoothly got them in the right lane and dropped speed but something was wrong--

The engine was still loud.

"What fucking now?" The driver whined, Joe could see her pumping her right foot.

The transmission was not going back into overdrive. The engine was still revving and the temp gauge was closing on the three-quarter mark again. The driver cut their speed to sixty.

"I don't think I should fuck with the shift lever---"

"No, don't." Joe and Jorge, almost in perfect unison.

"This isn't the end of the world, guys. If I keep it at sixty we should be okay, it'll just take longer."

The engine was still loud. The temp gauge had stopped rising and was steady at just below three-quarters. Outside it was 144 degrees. Joe pressed a palm to the glass and quickly dropped it. It was ten degrees hotter than when he had sought shelter in the Major Dollar. He could see that Jane was also studying the gauges. She would look down at her phone distractedly, not really looking at it, and then look up at the gauges and the road ahead.

"Tell us a story, writer," she said. "Get us the fuck out of this wretched car."

"I told you about the kid who got stabbed and the scientist...."

"And you don't have any more stories?" Jane said curtly. "Maybe something not so fucking depressing?"

Was she losing her shit? It didn't seem possible. Joe got the urge to hold her hand but feared the gesture would be rejected, possibly violently.

He thought of the way her breasts had felt, started getting an erection---

Yeah, like this the place for that sort of shit.

"I wish I did," Joe sighed. "Ever since I saw that kid get stabbed---"

"Three years ago," Jane looked over at him. "You've been focusing on that depressing shit for three years?"

The world is a fucking depressing place.

But he thought about her useless legs and his perspective and concerns and complaints about life seemed small and petty.

Jane was cracking her wrists and stretching her neck. Her anxiety had seemed to dissipate.

"What would you have done if you were that scientist?" Jorge asked. Jane looked back at him. The man in the third row didn't meet her gaze, looked out his own small window instead.

"If you could do something like provide endless freshwater or cure cancer but knew people around you would be tortured and killed--what would you do?" He continued.

Jane faced forward again and cued up the game on her phone.

"No fucking idea," she said flatly.

SEVENTEEN

Jane was rummaging through her bag. She pulled a pair of latex gloves out of a cardboard box and slipped them on.

"What are those for?"

The woman in the gloves looked over at Joe and shook her head before rummaging in her bag some more. She pulled out a gallon sized ziplock with a gun in it. Jane unzipped the bag, pulled the gun out, and looked it over. Before Joe could make any sense of or decide what he felt about what was happening Jane twisted around and shot Jorge twice in the head. The sound was surprisingly quiet, two pops. Jorge slumped against the left wall of the Hyundai. Blood and bits of flesh were all over the back window, Joe could smell them.

"Hey! You know the rules!" The driver, scowling into the rear view mirror.

Jane tossed the gun back with the body. She removed the gloves carefully and put them in the bag the pistol had been in. Pulling her phone up to her face, Jane pressed a button and waited until she heard a voice.

"It's done."

There was a humming soon accompanied by a clicking sound---was that coming from Jane's phone?

EIGHTEEN

Joe awoke with a start. The clicking and humming was coming from up front, from the box.

"I still think it could be a bomb." Jorge, his head still intact.

"Bombs don't usually make sounds." Jane, no fresh gunpower on her hand.

Joe looked over at her; his penis was still erect.

It's done.

They passed a flat tire that had been left on the side of the highway. The box became silent again.

NINETEEN

When the box had stopped making noise Jane winced as if bracing for an explosion. She looked over at Joe who smiled and mouthed *whew*. Jane smirked a little then went back to her phone.

"Normally I find the desert beautiful but there is like *nothing* as far as you can see."Jorge, drinking from a large bottle of water.

Hearing it slosh made Joe thirsty. He still had water but didn't want to have to piss---what would they do if someone needed to urinate? It was still a couple of hours to the City, probably more since the driver had to drop their speed. She was using her right hand to push buttons on the dash as she studied something on the dashboard.

"What's up, driver?

"Normally I have just enough gas to get from city to city with a little less than a gallon to spare. Without overdrive, I don't know if we'll make it."

I don't know if we'll make it. Joe struggled to keep his voice calm.

"Can't you just lower your speed until your RPMs in third gear match what they would have been in fourth at 70 miles per hour?"

"I could do that, but that would throw the schedule way off."

"Schedule? This car isn't going to make another trip."

"They'll have another car for me."

When the driver spoke again there was some rancor in her voice.

"I'll be assigned another piece of shit while they patch this one back together; it'll be back in service in a couple of days. They may not even fix Joe's window."

"Why do you work for such a shitty company?"

The driver rubbed the dash with the hand she had been pushing buttons with.

"I don't have a lot of options."

TWENTY

"This next pass is not as bad as the first one, but we may need to kill the AC and roll down the windows again."

Joe looked up at the dash, it was 138 outside. They were traveling between 45 and 50 miles per hour.

"At least we won't be passing anything at this speed," he said.

"You may be surprised," the driver replied.

The engine temp crossed the three-quarter mark. The driver rolled the three working windows down and killed the air conditioning.

"Sorry, guys; I hate this, too."

Joe studied her face in the rear view mirror. What were her eyes like behind those aviator sunglasses? Why did she feel as if she didn't have any other options?

Not like I am going to ask because I know the response: You know the rules!

On a steep curve the Hyundai kicked down into second and the engine got even louder--

Will it go back into third after this? Can we make it to the City with two gears? Will the transmission fall onto the pavement long after that?

And then the grade lessened and the car returned to third gear.

"Ah, shit," Jane said. "I don't think I've ever been so happy to hear a car shift."

Up ahead, a caravan of old RVs and school buses were struggling along at maybe twenty miles per hour, coronas of blue and white smoke surrounding the convoy.

"Shit," the driver muttered.

"Hey, don't worry about the schedule driver; we'll only be going twenty for ten minutes or so."

"I'm worried about going down the other side with all these ragtag vehicles; if one loses control it could take us with it."

She studied her rear view mirrors, licked her lips.

"I think we're good, if I keep it around 40 we shouldn't downshift."

47

The driver got into the left lane and began passing the caravan. Instead of appearing as downtrodden as their vehicles, the people leaning out the windows were laughing and smiling.

"Hey! Live free!"

"Enjoy life!"

"Fuck the power!"

Joe couldn't help but smile, even the driver was smiling a little--- And then the smile left her face and her hands gripped the wheel again.

An e-truck was coming up surprisingly fast and they were only halfway past the convoy.

"Uh, you may want to speed up…"

"If I hit the gas then we will definitely downshift."

The semi blared it's horn, the sound reminded Joe of evil laughter. He tightened his belt.

"We're almost past, maybe---"

And then the e-truck bumped them. As it was going thirty miles per hour faster than the Hyundai the impact knocked all four passengers around the cabin. The driver somehow maintained control and pulled in front of the convoy as the e-truck shot past. The people leaning out the windows had taken up a chant:

"Fuck you e-truck, fuck you fuck you fuck you e-truck!"

TWENTY-ONE

It was 118 degrees at the pass. The driver switched the air conditioning back on and rolled up the windows a minute later. Joe hadn't noticed that he was breathing furnace air, he kept thinking about the people leaning out of the shitty RVs and buses, how joyful they had been. Beginning the descent, they saw the City spread out below them: All the houses and streets and strip malls with Major Dollars seemed surreal after the emptiness and solitude of the desert. "We made it." Jorge, even without looking you could tell he was smiling.

"We still got traffic to get through," the driver had to burst his balloon.

With each exit scores of vehicles streamed onto the highway and the interstate grew from two lanes to three and then four and then five. Along the road were favelas made from tarps and grimy tents. The driver struggled to keep the car from downshifting into lower gears the transmission probably would get stuck in. The engine began heating up again. Even though it was nearly six when they finished the descent and the City surrounded them the outside air was still 129 degrees.

"Since we don't have any airflow I am going to keep the air on but we have to keep it on the lowest setting. I'll keep it on until we get all the way up to boiling."

No one said anything in response. With the air on low the heat quickly rendered them listless. Even Jane slumped against her door and stared at nothing. There was an exit every mile, making new lanes and bringing scores of cars onto the highway. It was rush hour and the driver struggled to maintain speed and then struggled not to come to a complete stop. If she left a space in front of the Hyundai, though, someone would squeeze in. The outside air had dropped to 127 degrees but the engine temp rose until it was right below boil over. Part of the problem was that the transmission was refusing to shift out of second.

They could only move along at thirty at most, but that was more than enough speed for the stop and go traffic.

After a few miles the engine temp was pegged at "H."
"How much further, driver?"
"A couple of miles until our exit."
There was a terrible sound from beneath the car and the engine began revving freely.
"Come on, we're almost there!"
The driver managed to get on the shoulder and moved the transmission level through all the gears; it finally caught in first.

TWENTY-TWO

Cars were lined up along the off ramp and parked tightly along the streets the entire mile it took to get to the pier. The Hyundai seemed to be working in low gear, roaring along at twenty-five miles per hour as a Suburban with what appeared to be twenty people in it tailgated and flashed the headlights. After a minute it shot past with every open window blooming with obscenities and angry gestures. Every space in the parking lot was full aside from nine empty handicapped spots---cars were even parked on the sidewalks. The driver parked in one of the handicapped spaces and then looked in the rear view mirror daring her passengers to protest. No one did, they just wanted the trip to be over. Before the driver shut off the engine Joe saw that it was 106 outside; it would probably get well below 100 once the sun was down, maybe it would get as low as 90. It felt weird to stand after so many hours in the car. Half stretching and half stepping, he went to the back hatch to get Jane's chair but the back of the car was too damaged to gain access.

"Hey---this door is completely fucked!"

"Yeah, we see; we're working it out up here," Jorge said.

A middle aged guy with a huge gut was walking towards the car.

"Hey!"

He stopped in his tracks when he saw Jorge wrestling the wheelchair out. The concerned citizen smiled and nodded before walking back the way he had come. Jorge pushed the wheelchair to the left side of the car and helped Jane into it.

"Just set my bag on my lap."

"Let's go down that pier over there," the driver said, pointing in the direction of a wooden finger stretching maybe an eighth of a mile into the sea.

"What about the box?"

The driver pushed a button on the key fob that locked the doors. The four of them made their way along the sidewalk, passing a bank of enormous vending machines filled with water and soda. Two

51

massive guards cradling riot guns watched over the queues leading up to them.

"Water is three times more expensive than soda."

None of the others had a response to Joe's observation.

Even at twilight the beach was so crowded you couldn't see any open sand. Children carved out small areas to play by making piles of the plastic debris that had washed up. Artists had made sculptures out of the plastic, one was an excellent likeness of Neptune that was over six feet tall. Where the sidewalk was blocked the driver Joe, and Jorge would pick up the chair and wrestle it past the obstruction. The pier had a lot of people on it but unlike the beach movement was easy even for Jane's chair. Joe watched the muscles in her arms as she turned the wheels. She caught him staring and he turned away quickly.

"I use to think about getting a sailboat." Jorge, adjusting the straps on his backpack, his face already glistening with sweat. "You set up some sort of desalination system, fish for food, keep some stores on the boat."

He held a hand up to his brow even though the sun was over the horizon.

"There is more to it than that….I don't know, I just daydream about it sometimes, just always being on the water, away from everything."

"You can't escape *everything*," Jane, stopping fast to avoid a child that had darted in front of her. "The world will find you wherever you go."

They reached the end of the pier. Joe rested his hands on the railing and looked down, wondering how deep the water was. He watched Jorge looking towards the horizon and imagined the other passenger on a boat with a happy expression on his face. The driver reached in her pocket, pulled the keys to the Hyundai out and tossed them over the edge. If they made it sound it was drowned out by the laughter of hundreds of children. Joe closed his eyes and savored the smell of the ocean air. Even with hundreds or even thousands of people surrounding them it was better than the closed in smell of the car--- And he was back in time; six people laughing as they walked towards a shitty car they were hoping would get them to the river. Joe was carrying a twelve pack of cheap beer and watching a flirtatious girl in a light, summer dress. The driver opened the trunk and made a joke that Joe would forget after that moment. He had laughed then because the joke was funny, he remembered that much. One of his friends put a twelve pack in the trunk and Joe followed suit. Standing on the edge of the pier with his eyes closed he could see that the trunk was a mess: Old clothes. Half full bottles of oil and steering fluid and antifreeze. Only one thing stood out among all the detris, a box neatly wrapped box in brown paper

DO NOT
ReaD
Any FurtHer

The story you just read--*our* story--was perfect. We believe the author understands that and yet he has continued writing about us, going deeper into our lives, motivations, and so on. Those stories are on the pages that follow. None of us can see a valid reason for the author doing so and strongly suggest that you do not read any further. Our stories do not need to be told at greater length, our secrets revealed. You do not need to read about the experiences that led us to that journey through the desert or what happened to us after we stood on that pier. Please do not read any further. Close the book, set it down, and walk away.

Jane

Jorge

Joe

The Driver

Part Two:
Bud and Lou

ONE

She walked out further into the desert, closer to the moment of her death.
It had been 133 right before the explosion---how long could you survive out in the open in such heat? How long had she been out there, anyway? The woman in the desert had no idea; her ears were ringing and nothing seemed real.

There was one sip of water left in her canteen. She understood that whether she drank it or poured it onto the hardpan it made no difference: That one sip would not save her. Maybe it would have been better if she had died with the others; at least she wouldn't have died alone.

The woman walked parallel to the road a hundred yards from the asphalt: Close enough to watch for and wave to friendly vehicles, far enough to be out of sight of the enemy should they pass. The road would lead to a town with one of their guard stations. The odds of reaching it in that heat---even if her canteen had been full---were low. All she could do was keep walking.

The hard earth below her boots was as hot as a car door handle on a summer day; Sergeant had told them that the day they arrived in the merciless desert. Why then could she imagine curling up on it and going to sleep? Something was drying tacky on her face. Probably blood. Hers? Unknown.

Everytime she tried to give herself a pep talk, tried to be strong, the soldier was back in the destroyed Humvee with the smell of burning. It wasn't just scorched machine she had smelled, it was organic things as well. That was as far as she dared think about it. She paused on the hardpan, going back to the moments after it had happened: Her hands were on the wheel, eight and four, not gripping it just holding it gentle. Staring through the space the windshield had

taken. There was a weight on her lap. When she regained some of her senses the woman determined it was a foot. Whenever she tried to give herself a pep talk the weight of that foot or the sight of the body parts scattered around the Humvee would come back to her---How was she supposed to be strong? How?
She shook off her doubts and walked on.

TWO

A vehicle was moving down the road. From where she stood the vehicle was too small to determine if it was friend or foe. There wasn't much time left, her body told her that. What if it was one of their patrols? Could that be a Humvee? Should she wave or fire her sidearm? What if it was the people who had left the bomb for them? What would they do to her? Whatever it was wouldn't be good. The vehicle was stopping. The woman couldn't decide whether to drop to the ground and make herself small or---
The vehicle was turning, it was coming her way.

The woman in the desert pulled her sidearm and took the safety off with the weapon pointed at the hardpan. She understood that she did not have the element of surprise on her side and that anyone out there would be armed. Would it be good to at least take a stand? Die in a firefight? Maybe. If the enemy captured her they would surely rape her. Sergeant had told her that over and over: *If you are taken, Haj will fuck you when he is not torturing you.*
She had her finger over the trigger. The vehicle was now close enough to see it was a Toyota Hilux. There were two men in the cab and four others standing in the bed with rifles.
This is when it happens: They see I have a gun, yell some Arabic shit, and aim their rifles at me.
Would it be quick or would she suffer? She had seen people sprayed with a dozen shots live for hours in agony---
One of the men in the back was yelling. She didn't know enough Arabic to make it out but whatever he was saying was harsh, harsh as the hardpan she was about to die on.
"Drop gun! Drop gun!" One of the men in the bed was yelling that. That was the moment, her chance: Either she could raise her sidearm and try and take out a couple of them or---
The woman felt the gun drop from her hand, heard the mild thud as it landed on the dead earth.

Her sidearm was at her feet and her arms were going up, she was surrendering---

If you are taken, Haj will fuck you when he is not torturing you.

One of the men ran to her, cupping a breast as he checked her for other weapons.

This is how it begins. At least if I had tried to fight it would be over by now.

Another man had run over, he yelled something at the first man---asshole? She knew a few swear words and could have sworn the second Haj said *asshole*. The second Haj was forcing his canteen into her right hand.

"You drink fast, you get sick."

She looked from the canteen up to his face.

"You speak English?"

He grabbed her left arm hard enough to bruise and led her towards the truck. She took a couple sips of water; it tasted like dirt, it was glorious. She climbed into the back of the truck. The men were all around her, smelling of sweat and cooking and dirty clothes. She was powerless, they could do whatever they wanted.

THREE

The soldier tried to remain standing but the road was too rough and the driver too jerky with the accelerator and brake. She nearly fell and the men laughed. They stood with ease. A space was made for her to sit on one of the wheel wells. Her posture was erect. From the waist up she was standing at attention, determined not to show weakness. Inside---

Inside she was imagining a prison rudely made of concrete. There would be a cell with a dirt floor shared with men who would rape her and other rooms where they would shove things under her nails or attach car batteries to her nipples and genitals and---

Stop it. This is what They want. This is what the enemy wants: Fear.
A firm voice said that in her head, a strong voice that would get her through any ordeal---

No, the voice was a hollow lie.

They arrived at a village with dirt streets and squat concrete buildings with tin roofs. No one was on the street, which seemed strange. The Hilux drove to the other end of the village and stopped in front of a modern looking house. It was small but could have fit in back in the soldier's hometown. One of the men was talking to her, pointing his rifle from her to the front door of the house. She nodded and climbed out of the back of the truck. One of the men from the cab had gone to the front door and knocked on it. Another man had answered it, he nodded at the man from the truck and then smiled at the woman. It was a kind looking smile and he had kind eyes---

Yeah, and one of his buddies blew us up. Think of the foot, think of whatever those guts were you stepped in when walking away from the wreak; these people are not kind. This is the "good cop." He will ask some questions and when he doesn't get what he wants the "bad cop" will show up.

"Please, come in."

His English was unaccented. No, the accent was slight but familiar---was it a Southern accent? Maybe Georgia or South

Carolina? Her host---*Haji*---was somewhere in his late thirties, overweight, below average in height, and wearing khakis with a green and white striped polo shirt.

And that would be the shape of a gun where his shirt drapes over his khakis. Kind eyes, my ass.

The living room was cool, so different from the open desert it nearly made her ill. The man put a hand on her arm and gently led her to a chair, she was too weak to resist. The chair was next to a table where there were two glasses and a pitcher of water with condensation on the outside. She wanted a glass of that water as much as she had ever wanted anything but willed herself not to reach for it. The prisoner placed one hand palm down on the table as the other reached in her undershirt to pull out her dog tags and lay them on the table. The man picked up the tags and examined them for a few seconds before setting them on the table in front of her.

"Kelsey, my name is Bud." He poured her a glass of water. "You appear to be suffering from heat stroke, I suggest you sip this."

"What is this place? Is this where you process me?"

He appeared confused so she continued.

"Where you take my information before taking me to jail."

"You will not be taken anywhere, this is where you will stay."

At least there's air conditioning.

There were also two doors; who knew what was behind them.

Good cop, bad cop. Nice room, pain room.

"There is blood on your uniform and face, Kelsey. I will send a female medic in to look you over, deal with any wounds---"

"What is this?"

"What do you mean?"

He already knows. This nice guy/nice place thing is to open me up--they must think I know something.

"This...this is not what I was expecting..."

That's all Kelsey had: She was weak and her ears were still ringing and she kept seeing the guts she had stepped in.

"You need to rest, Kelsey. The medic will be in soon."

FOUR

Kelsey heard the deadbolt click after Bud walked out the front door. It was a nice place, nicer than the condo she lived in back home, but it was still a prison. She struggled to her feet, determined to map the layout of her "cell." The table, chairs surrounding it, and grey couch looked as if they were from IKEA. There were a couple of still lifes on the wall: Flowers and a harbor surrounded by small whitewashed houses; the paintings appeared to have been stolen from a Best Western. The room was eight paces square. One door opened to a bathroom like any bathroom back home down to the Kohler fixtures. The other door opened to a room with a full sized bed, shelves, and a flatscreen mounted on the wall. There were clothes on the shelf: Khakis. T-shirt. Bra. Underwear. Sneakers. Kelsey picked them up, they were her sizes. Before she could guess what that meant or determine what she felt the guest heard the front door opening. It was someone in an ankle length dress, presumably a woman. Only her eyes and bridge of her nose showed through the veil wrapped around her head. The eyes looked angry.

She looks like she wants to kill me---

Maybe this is the bad cop. Maybe she has all her bad cop tools in that black duffel.

The woman was, angry eyes or not, a couple of inches shorter than Kelsey. Was she trained in hand to hand combat?

"Take off your clothes." Her English was rough but understandable. Kelsey just looked at her.

I take her down and grab her gun and...then what? I don't imagine there are a lot of friendly faces outside that door.

And she was still weak from wandering in the desert and the ringing in her ears and stepping in the guts of someone she had considered a close friend…

"Look---this does not matter to me, get inflections for all I care.. " Kelsey began taking her clothes off. Pulling a sleeve down there was the sensation of something small but sharp moving. She winced, the medic got closer to look.

"Yes, probably shrapnel. I will pull it out."

The medic was rough as she pulled out a few pieces of shrapnel and addressed some burns and a deep cut on one side of Kelsey's face. After she had left, the guest/prisoner dressed in clean clothes. Still weak, she sat at the table and sipped water. The deadbolt was working again, Bud had returned.

"Bud...I take it that's not a common name around here."

The smile left his eyes for a moment; it was only a moment but it was enough.

Yeah, maybe there's a bad cop lurking around in there, after all.

"What would you prefer to call me?"

"How about your real name?"

Bud chuckled, shifting his attention to the tablet he was carrying.

"Okay, tell me this," she continued. "Do you process every soldier like me in a place like this?"

He looked at her without a smile.

"No." The truth, that was clear.

"Why am I different?"

Bud sat at the table. The smile returned but it was less generous, there was some *smirk* to it.

"Kelsey...like you I am following orders. They told me that you had been picked up and that you were to be brought here and treated like a guest. Your wishes for TV shows or food are to be complied with---whatever you want."

"Whatever I want?"

"Yes."

"How about a ride back to the base?"

He chuckled and grabbed the pitcher to fill himself a glass of water.

FIVE

Maybe I died, maybe this is where we end up…
She was sitting on the couch with that thought going in a loop despite her best efforts.
How else do you explain all this? Captured soldiers don't end up in places like this. Besides, how could I have come out of the explosion relatively unhurt when the others were blown apart?
Kelsey jumped off the couch. She slapped herself and then pinched a hand until it bled.
"This is some fucking head game, nothing else. Psy ops or something."
Exercises---exercises would get the blood flowing and the blood flowing would bring the brain back to life. She did burpees, paced a bit, then did push ups using the armrest of the couch. A camera in the corner reminded her that They were watching. She willed herself not to care.

In the first hours food or hunger were the last thing on Kelsey's mind. When the light began softening outside her stomach began making fists. As instructed, she knocked on the front door. The guest heard the deadbolt a few minutes later followed by Bud's smiling face.
Why are you smiling? Your smile doesn't fit this situation--
Maybe that's the point, maybe your smile and the new couch and the air conditioning are all part of whatever this is.
"Did you think of something you'd like?"
"When you say anything do you mean *anything* food related?"
"Yes." His smile had thinned, something about her question amused him.
There is more to you than kindness. My perception is that I do not want to experience whatever that is.
"Does it have to be halal?"
Bud laughed, it seemed genuine.
"No---"

"Isn't it *haram* for you guys to even cook some things?"

"Please do not concern yourself, Kelsey."

Something in his eyes, something about the whole conversation--

This is some sort of set-up, a test or an experiment or something.

"Okay, then I'd like a cheeseburger and fries."

"No problem. What would you like on it?"

"Light mayo and mustard." She thought about how barren the desert they had driven through looked and added. "Lettuce and tomato."

He just looked at her for a moment or two; his eyes betrayed a computer hidden somewhere making calculations.

"No problem," Bud replied.

An hour passed according to a clock mounted above the bathroom door. Was it accurate or just a prop? The light was dimming outside and the clock was claiming it was half past seven; that seemed about right.

The deadbolt, Bud had returned. He was carrying a styrofoam box the size of a large book.

Just popped out to Sonic for your burger...

"Is there anything else?" He asked.

The kind smile again, maybe his bosses had been watching their last interaction and had offered some coaching---

She can tell you are hiding something, push the computer down to the sub basement.

"No, thank you." There was no need to be impolite.

"If you need water there is a secondary faucet in the bathroom. That water is filtered and cooled."

She looked right at him, eye to eye.

"Wow, you guys thought of everything."

He didn't break eye contact, his smile didn't falter.

"Enjoy your meal, Kelsey."

SIX

Kelsey didn't open the styrofoam box until after Bud had left. It smelled delicious, the tomato appeared ripe and the lettuce was crisp---

She thought of the desert surrounding them, how it went on for miles and miles and miles in any direction…

"Fuck it."

The guest took a bite. It was as delicious as it smelled as were the fries. Her eating picked up momentum until all the food was gone aside from a fragment of tomato in the bottom of the box. She found herself staring at it, a red glob---

And she was back in time: Staggering out of the Humvee, slipping on something…

They are watching. They are always watching.

Kelsey shut the styrofoam box and walked into the bedroom. She made a show of pulling back the covers as if checking the bed for cleanliness. There was a camera in there, as well. Her only privacy was in the bathroom unless there was a well hidden camera; she didn't want to think about that.

Looking in the styrofoam box, the red fragment---

Whose name was attached to the guts had she slipped on? Jacob? Todd? Devon? Were they from the same body the foot had come from?

Something was coming, emotions big enough to tear down cities with merciless waves---

Kelsey forced them out of her mind. They were watching, They were always watching.

The only window was in the door leading to the back patio. The patio was one pace deep and four in length. It was still hot but evening had made it bearable. A cement wall surrounded the patio, one taller than Kelsey even with her arms outstretched. The heat became unpleasant despite the darkness; she went inside after a few minutes.

Kelsey took the measurements of each room, using her paces and then her outstretched arms. She noted each piece of furniture and fixture. When she tired of that the guest/prisoner sat on the edge of the bed and attempted to piece together where she might be. How far had they driven out on patrol? Why hadn't she been watching the odometer? They had driven south from the base for an hour at around forty miles per hour. Forty miles. What about after the capture? She had been too out of it.

"Come on, get your shit together."

Kelsey lay back on the bed. It was comfortable. Where had they found such a comfortable bed?

SEVEN

She was late for work, running through a Major Dollar looking for something for lunch. She was pretty sure the coolers were in the back so she jogged down the aisles. They ended at a beige, cement wall with Arabic writing on it. She was going to be late; where were the coolers? Maybe if she followed the wall…

Kelsey came out of the dream. Was she awake? This didn't look like a place she usually woke up in---
The apartment. Bud. Being captured. The explosion---
Fully clothed, the dull ache of healing wounds under bandages.
Kelsey was aware that she smelled. The last shower had been before leaving base the previous morning. She looked over at the clothes on the shelf. Hadn't there only been one set of clothes before? Now the shelf was full of identical pants and shirts and underwear. All in her size. That the bra fit perfectly was the most disconcerting part.
This is going to remain a mystery for a while, I can either be dirty or clean in my confusion.
Kelsey grabbed a set of clothes and carried it to the bathroom. She started to undress but stopped. With only her shirt off she stood on the toilet and scanned the seams where the walls met the ceiling for cameras. She found herself fixating on the patterns in the paint: Workmen. Definitely work*men* in that place. What had they thought when they were building that apartment? It probably was a lot nicer than the other places in the village. What had they told their families? Or, was the work done by soldiers trained to keep their mouths shut? Starting to feel vertigo, she climbed off the toilet and removed the rest of her clothes.

EIGHT

That first morning had been the hardest. In the barracks her commanders set the routine; now she was on her own, untethered to any commands or obligations. Kelsey sat on the bed clean but ill at ease. Everything seemed comfortable, not the sort of place she had imagined was her destination when the truck full of armed men had confronted her. Kelsey was struggling not to show anxiety even as fear erected tall buildings with neon signs inside her---she had imagined a rude prison with dirt floors and cinderblock walls; she imagined torture and rape---

Instead the men had taken her to an apartment nicer than the one she had lived in back home. Bud had shown up with his kind face and offers of *whatever she wanted*. This was confusing and in some ways worse than the dirt floored jail she had built in her imagination; was this just a temporary place They were keeping her? A trick to lower her defenses?

A knock on the door. Why were they knocking instead of just coming in as they had the previous day? Should she just sit on the bed and see if whomever it was used the key? The knocking stopped. A moment later, the deadbolt turned. Were they waiting to see that she was dressed? No, the cameras would have already told them that. It was Bud with a carafe and two cups for the coffee inside it. In the coming days she would determine that he showed up precisely fifteen minutes after she finished dressing following her morning shower. That first morning, he had made polite inquiries about whether or not she approved of the shower.

"The pressure was kind of low but the temperature was nearly ideal."

"Oh, I apologize about the pressure. We do not have very good pressure out here."

And where is that, Bud?

"Hey...would it be possible to get a razor?"

He looked confused---maybe that was something women did not talk to men about in their culture.

But, that accent...he must have spent some time in the U.S. Maybe he didn't have a girlfriend or maybe they didn't talk about that shit.
Do I really wanna talk about shaving myself with him?
After a few moments it was clear he understood her question. Bud looked down at the table and wouldn't meet her eyes the rest of his time there.

"Ah, I am sorry but no razors. We could, ah, have a woman come in and shave you if you'd like."

Kelsey shook her head. Bud nodded and the conversation was mercifully over.

NINE

Four days passed. Four days of polite conversations that went nowhere, four days of *Better Call Saul*, four days of them bringing her whatever food Kelsey requested. She had tested them: Mexican food. Thai. Italian. English pub food. Each time they had met the challenge at least acceptably.

Her fourth afternoon softened bringing shadows. Kelsey sat on the edge of the bed staring at the shelves and then looking over at the door to the patio. There was no lock on it, just an antique looking brass knob. She stared at it knowing They were staring at her through the camera. Kelsey got up and tested the knob; it was loose, had a lot of texture. She could feel the heat outside through the metal. And then she was turning it, and then she was on the back patio where it smelled like cement and the heat was a weight making it difficult to stand. Kelsey walked to the wall and looked up. What was it, ten feet high? She went back inside and got a chair. Standing on it K could almost reach the top of the wall. What if she asked for some books? Placing the chair back at the table, Kelsey started thinking of books she could ask them for---epic novels, maybe; large books that would give her the one to two feet she needed.

The next day Bud had shown up with a tablet under his arm. He looked sad or maybe disappointed. Bud had motioned Kelsey over to the tablet so she could be shown footage of her experiment with the chair which cut to drone footage of the patio and what lay beyond, miles of open desert. Unforgiving, a hundred-forty degree desert exactly the same as the place They had found her in/rescued her from. A raven swooped into frame and then disappeared. When the footage ended Bud left without saying a word.

He had not brought her coffee. Kelsey wasn't sure why she felt bad for making Bud upset, the only thing she knew for sure was that she missed her coffee.

A knock on the door, the sound of the deadbolt, and a tall slender man with an unhappy face walked in carrying an AK-47. He wasn't pointing it at her just cradling it to his chest but she understood that could change.

That thing with the chair--is that going to change everything? Is this the Bad Cop?

The man set the gun against the door frame and grabbed something on the other side of the door: A carafe and a single cup. He carried them to the table and set them down. This man was not trying to be friendly, he was clearly uncomfortable with serving Kelsey.

To Bud I am "a guest," to this guy I am a prisoner.

"I was told to bring you coffee."

His English was heavily accented. Unlike Bud he had probably picked it up in a training camp or madrasa or something.

"Thank you." There was no need to be rude. "Do you have a name?"

"I was told that you can call me Lou."

There was no softness, no playfulness; Lou was uncomfortable around her and possibly did not like the *infidel* in his midst. He did not pour her coffee. Kelsey filled her own cup and looked over his shoulder at the rifle against the wall. He caught her looking and his expression sent a clear message:

You do not want to underestimate me.

She nodded, took a sip of her coffee.

"I will leave now," he said. "Please knock on the door if you need or want anything."

"Yeah."

Lou was staring at her as if he wanted to ask or was expecting something.

"So...Bud was hurt by my standing on the chair?"

"Hurt?"

"His feelings, I made him feel bad?"

Lou looked over at his rifle then back at her. There was a new expression on his face and talking about Bud had brought it out. It was a softness---

They're close friends, maybe more than friends...don't they kill people for that out here?

"Bud has been very kind to you, and you returned that kindness by plotting."

Plotting? Well, yeah, duh--I am your fucking prisoner; of course I am testing the boundaries.

Instead of saying that Kelsey placed her palms down on the table and looked up at Lou.

"I'm sorry I was rude to Bud. Please share my apology with him."

Lou picked up his rifle and cradled it again. He looked at the floor, looked over at the painting of the flowers, did not look at Kelsey.

"I can do that."

TEN

After Kelsey finished her coffee she walked into the bedroom and looked up at the camera. Who was watching? Bud? Was he still upset at her?

Why the fuck should I care? He's nothing more than a prison guard. She walked over to the antique brass knob and touched it. Warm growing hot; even with the awning over the patio. Bud was never sweaty nor was Lou, clearly they had air conditioning, as well. Conscious of making things worse, Kelsey walked away from the door to the patio. She sat on the bed and thought of the drone flying over an endless desert.

And I was going to just hop over that wall and saunter off. Yeah, that was well thought out.

Until They decided what to do with her at least Kelsey was somewhere clean and cool with good food.

It's also a prison, never forget that. You saw that AK-47, that was not a toy. You are their prisoner.

She walked in the bathroom and studied herself in the mirror.

It may be a prison but it's nicer than the barracks or our condo back home that I shared with three people. What really is a prison? Working your ass off, getting in debt just to live and go to school while working a shitty job just to keep your head above water? Being in the military where you are in danger and people scream at you all day? Which prison is the worse one?

"This is how they get you."

She said that out loud but softly.

ELEVEN

On the sixth night Kelsey asked for Mexican food. It was good, tasty enough that she could imagine Mexicans had made it, but the effect on her guts wasn't quite as enjoyable. Sitting on the toilet with the minutes passing, she reached over and pinched the paper on the roller; it was good stuff, definitely better than in the barracks. Where could they even *find* that out there? She looked at the opposite wall, at the ceiling, at the floor. There was a dark spot on the linoleum. Kelsey leaned forward to study it: Blood, you could tell by the cracks on the edges. Someone had lost blood in there and it hadn't been her. Had it? No, the medic had treated her in the living room. Maybe a wound rinsing left blood in the shower but not there in front of the toilet. Who had lost blood in there and why?

TWELVE

Stepping from the bathroom on the seventh day she saw color for the first time in a week: Blue. Nine flowers with their long stems leading into an emerald green vase. No, it wasn't a vase. Her memory turned wheels to make sense of the curves: It was a bottle, an old 7-Up bottle. Where had They even gotten an old 7-Up bottle? Did They even have 7-Up in their shops? After weeks of beiges and other earth tones the blue and green was startling. Emotions surprised her but she didn't allow them to overwhelm her: They were watching. They acted kindly and left her flowers but she *knew* They were watching for any sort of weakness; that's what enemies do. The flowers were just another test, a man wearing a blindfold running his fingers over a wall looking for an opening.

Bud was back that morning with the carafe and two cups acting like nothing had ever happened.
"Did you sleep well, Kelsey?"
"Yeah, thank you for the flowers."
She said that looking directly in his eyes sleuthing for a reaction. He met her gaze but revealed nothing. His warm smile became a gentle smirk as Bud poured coffee for both of them.
"I am certain Lou did not drink coffee with you, he does not like your American coffee."
"I don't think he likes *me*, either."
Bud looked over his shoulder at the camera up on the wall and then looked back at her. Was that to let her know Lou was watching?
"Do you like us, Kelsey?"
She looked into her cup for a safe answer. Finding none, she took a sip.
"I like you, Bud, I'm just confused."
He took a sip from his own cup and shrugged in the direction of the door.
"If I left the front door unlocked and did not stop you from leaving, would you?"

She looked over at the door, unsure if it was a test and if so what the rules were.

I would die out there. Even if I was given a couple of canteens, even if I went at night it would still be a hundred degrees and I have no idea where I am. The road signs are in Arabic and the War has been shifting so fast I have no idea what areas are friendly and which ones aren't.

If she was to answer *no*, then she technically wasn't a prisoner.

If she were to answer *yes*, and Bud called her on it and opened the door---

Kelsey looked into her cup and a moment later took another drink.

THIRTEEN

She was back in the Humvee. The other three were laughing at some in-joke. She saw a burned out sedan a couple hundred yards off the road, they were close---
Kelsey swerved hard around where her memory was telling her the IED had been.
"What the fuck, corporal?!"
"You still hungover or something?"
Laughter. She had to smile herself; they were safe. She had saved them.
Up ahead was a tell tale dark spot on the road where something had recently been buried. A child with a phone was watching them from nearby.
It was too late to react.

Kelsey sat up in the bed. She had been clutching the pillow as she dreamt. They had seen it, had probably nodded and made notes that she was having a nightmare or displaying some other form of weakness. Sleep was gone from the moment her eyes opened. The dream had stirred up emotions she wanted to keep private, the sound of her friends laughing as if they were still alive. That was a great moment; if she could have lived those moments on a loop forever that would have made her happy. But the moments were gone, only to be played back in cruel dreams.

Later she did her exercises in the other room, some burpees followed by a set of push-ups, and worked on getting her mind clear. Lou had been there with Bud the previous morning. There had been a look between them, a look that fit into a category that wasn't friends or army buddies---
Don't they kill people in this country for being queer?
Lou had been warmer with her. Still distant, awkwardly mannered, but he had complimented her hair. It wasn't a come on. No, not after

that look he had given Bud. She found herself liking them in those rare moments she let her guard down...

Bud and Lou are not my friends. They killed the others...

Had they? The situation had started with a bomb blowing up their vehicle but--- although the possibility existed---the connection with Bud and his partners wasn't confirmed.

They found me before I died of exposure or thirst or whatever. I was out there, what, a couple of hours? They had to be close, watching; the bomb was probably their doing or the work of people they're in league with.

That strengthened her resolve. Kelsey did a set of crunches and contemplated what she knew about her situation. Escape? Where would she go? She was deep in unfriendly territory, didn't even know the language. Rescue, that was the only hope. Her people would find the wreckage and note it was a body short, they would move out in all directions until that body was located.

What if They hid the wreckage? If They can get me whatever food I like and know what detergent we use back home They probably know about the tracking devices placed on the vehicles and how to remove them. I could be stuck here for years, maybe the rest of my life.

No, thinking like that was counterproductive.

Kelsey took a deep breath and began doing squats.

FOURTEEN

Lou brought the coffee the following morning. His rifle was on a sling and the barrel tapped the table as he set the carafe and single cup down. He leaned the gun next to the door and sat across from Kelsey as she drank her coffee.

"Supposed to be very hot today; they say it could be sixty degrees."

"Sixty? Celsius, right?"

He made a face, pulled out his phone.

They have signal out here. She made a note but kept her face neutral.

"Ah, one hundred-forty degrees fahrenheit."

She took a sip of her coffee and could have sworn she tasted cinnamon.

"Any word from the Commander?"

"Pardon?"

"About what you guys are going to do with me."

He just looked at her.

Maybe this *is the torture, these uncomprehending looks…*

"Come on, Lou...we all know this game, your Commander has plans for me, maybe trade with my Commander for one of your guys---I don't know, there's always a plan in these situations."

Lou looked down at the table, he almost looked...*hurt*?

"Do you not like it here? Haven't we given you whatever you want?"

"It's not that. Come on...let's be real, I am your prisoner."

Lou looked over his shoulder at the camera on the wall and then back in Kelsey's general direction while avoiding her gaze.

"I am sorry that you see it that way, Kelsey. Did Bud not offer to leave the door unlocked for you a few days ago?"

"Yes---"

"Then...how can you suggest that you are a prisoner?"

"You and I know," she nodded towards the camera. "We *all* know that without help getting to an American base my odds are not good out there. Especially at sixty degrees."

He looked at her. It was the first time Lou looked at her dead on without any awkwardness. It could have been revealing but she had no idea what she was seeing. Lou looked off to his left and nodded, pushed back the chair, and walked over to the front door.

"Please let us know what you would like to eat when you decide."

After nodding he grabbed his rifle and walked out the door.

FIFTEEN

That night her sleep was dreamless. She climbed out of bed and studied the dried blood on the floor of the bathroom as the shower warmed up.

Maybe it's from the last "guest." This was where They killed them, They thought they cleaned it well but---

Not helping. Not helping at all.

Bud brought the coffee that morning. He looked tired; no kind smile, no inquiries about how she was feeling.

"Having a bad morning, Bud?"

He looked up at her, clearly attempting to smile his usual smile and failing.

"Have we done something wrong? Have we offended you, Kelsey?"

"No...I could tell Lou's feelings were hurt yesterday and I am sorry for that."

*"I'm sorry for that"--what the fuck? They are holding you **prisoner**.*

"I believe you see this situation in the wrong way."

"Bud...Lou props a gun at the door, I can see you have a gun under your shirt. Can we just be real about this? Please?"

The smile left his face. He poured coffee into the two cups.

"This situation is not as simple as prisoner and captors."

"It isn't?" *I already sensed that.*

"We found you in the desert--"

"Bud, no offense but how do I know you didn't blow up our Humvee?"

He just looked at her.

"You do not. Maybe we did, maybe we didn't, that is also irrelevant…"

"No, it is *very* relevant because it means you killed people I am very close to. It means you are hunting American soldiers."

"And why would we do that?" Bud smirked; it wasn't his usual playful smirk, there was darkness to it.

Yeah, yeah, because we invaded your fucking country and killed a lot of people---you got me there. I'm sure you guys have been happy with the sick dictators that have been murdering your countrymen by the score for generations.

"You and Lou have been very kind to me, I just want to know what's going to happen to me, you know?"

He took a sip of his coffee without his eyes leaving hers.

"You will know when we know."

SIXTEEN

That night she asked for macaroni and cheese. Kelsey wanted bacon
in it but feared it would be seen as a taunt. The darkness in Bud's
smirk---it was clear that he was close to his limit with her but *why?*
Why was asking about what they planned to do with her making
them so irate? Urinating, she became fixated on the feeling of the
stretched elastic against her calves. Where did they get women's
underwear? Did the local women wear the same kind as they did in
the United States? Kelsey had no idea. She looked down at drop of
dried blood---
You will know when we know.

The macaroni and cheese was amazing. No bacon but they had
crumbled bar-be-que potato chips onto it. As she ate Kelsey felt
happy and had no idea where the happiness was coming from. When
was the last time she had felt happy---
*Out on the road. All of us laughing, right before I spotted that kid
with the phone.*
The happiness was gone in an instant. She wanted to throw her bowl
against the wall, scream, probably cry, but They were watching.
They were always watching. She would not gift them her weakness.
Kelsey made herself smile a little and kept eating.

SEVENTEEN

A few hours later K was lying in bed watching *Better Call Saul*. In the background of one of the scenes, a busker was playing an Oasis song on her guitar but not singing. Without the words and vocal melody, she couldn't place the name of the song by the time the scene ended. It was lying under the covers when she recognized the song.

The first dream found her driving through a desert in some beat ass car; a Hyundai SUV. It was hot, the readout on the dash claimed it was 138 degrees. There were three people in the back: An Asian woman somewhere in her twenties. A stocky Hispanic guy that was maybe a decade older. A White dude somewhere around the same age that was anonymous looking aside from having golden colored eyes. On the seat next to her was a box that was maybe two feet square and wrapped in brown paper. Whomever had wrapped it had done a professional job. They hadn't even used tape; it must have been held together with some sort of glue. There was a gun in her door. Kelsey knew her orders: Deliver the others to the City across the desert. Ensure their safety but ensure the safety of the box even more. If anyone tries to fuck with the box kill them.
And then someone was complaining, bitching about the heat or something, their voice shrill like a child---

The flatscreen had been left on. *Better Call Saul* had concluded and now there were a bunch of children in a park. Arab looking children. They were playing and squealing with joy and then---
A fireball and all the children were dead and the swingsets and slides were charred and melted. Kelsey started sobbing, she couldn't help it.
You fuckers--like I had anything to do with any of this shit! I enlisted after the bombings; you fuckers attacked us first!
The screen went black. Kelsey felt naked and struggled to rein her emotions in but knew They had already seen her crying and that

trying to cover it up was meaningless. She stood up and looked around the room.

"I would never kill a fucking child, you assholes! I am in not in charge, I just---"

Follow orders? Was that really going to be the next two words out of my mouth?

She sat on the edge of the bed feeling more defeated that she had felt in at least thirteen days.

EIGHTEEN

The next morning, a new man showed up with her coffee. He had only brought one cup.

Here he is, the Bad Cop...

But Kelsey didn't get that vibe off him. He was handsome and had a certain suaveness down to his well-tailored suit.

Maybe this is the Commander, maybe now I get some answers.

"Good morning, Kelsey."

"Are you the Commander?"

He laughed easily, it felt genuine.

"No, no. You may call me Jerry, like the comic Jerry Lewis."

"Jerry Lewis?"

"You do not know your own comedians? He was very popular in your country."

"No, sorry, never heard of him..."

"Some people call him a comic genius, I am not so sure."

"And yet you took his name..."

"Or perhaps it was assigned to me as Bud and Lou were assigned their names."

"I'm just Kelsey."

He motioned to her cup. She nodded and he filled it. His movements were elegant, almost feminine.

"Where is Bud?"

"Sick. Very bad case of influenza. His room smells of vomit."

Room. New information. Kelsey kept a straight face.

"That's too bad."

"Are you sure that you feel that way? Being our *prisoner* and all?"

"Come on, you guys need to stop being offended by that..."

"Why? Does this seem like a prison to you? Have we not offered every kindness, every amenity you could ask for?"

"This is not my home, you are not my people---"

"And what did your people do to you?" Anger just underneath the cologne and handsomeness and civility. "Lied to you, conned you into coming here to kill my people for no reason."

87

He was leaning forward a little. She wouldn't let herself be pushed back, placing her hands on top of the table and leaning forward herself.

"You killed a bunch of people back home."

Even if her voice was firm Kelsey felt a hollowness to her reply. Even at the height of her patriotic fervor she had doubts about the whole situation. Jerry was watching her very closely, she felt him pull his anger back into wherever he kept it safe.

"This gets us nowhere, Kelsey. Perhaps we should avoid the bigger picture."

"Whatever, I just want to know what's going to happen to me."

"I do not know and that is my honest answer. We have been instructed to show you every courtesy until the Commander has made a decision."

"Have you ever met him? This is where you look over your shoulder at the camera and then back at me."

Jerry smiled and refilled her cup after noting that it was empty.

After Jerry left she started her exercises beginning with burpees.
We have been instructed to show you every courtesy until the Commander has made a decision.
Kelsey thought of the minutes before the explosion: They had been laughing, some inside joke erased by the trauma.
She thought about the dream with the box on the seat next to her; Kelsey had the odd but undeniable feeling the dream was set in the future.

NINETEEN

Kelsey had asked them to bring her a cheeseburger and fries for dinner along with a six pack of Coors. Lou had brought it and for the first time did not have his rifle with him.

"I apologize but we could not get Coors this quickly; I hope Budweiser is acceptable."

"Yeah, no problem. Thanks."

And then a realization: *Maybe they got the beer bombing and/or over-running a forward base. Maybe they got all the food and drink they've been giving me by killing other Americans---*

Or, this is all one big ruse, one head fuck courtesy of the U.S. Army; that would explain why Bud and Lou get upset when I say that I am the prisoner.

Lou didn't seem to notice her contemplation. He looked as if he was coming down with something.

"You getting what Bud has?"

Lou looked over at her warily.

"Honestly, my throat is starting to get scratchy, as well." Kelsey added quickly---*maybe he caught me picking up on that look he gave Bud.* "Maybe tomorrow I will ask for soup. If I do you'll know I'm sick because I hate soup."

He smiled at that.

"I would suggest not drinking all six beers, then. If you need tea or anything else please knock."

"I will."

She ate all of her food and drank three beers while watching more of *Better Call Saul*. The burger wasn't sitting well and Kelsey accepted that she was coming down with something.

The first dream placed her in a desert city. Maybe it was Phoenix or maybe it was Las Vegas. She was standing in a covered parking lot with dozens of crappy looking cars, the Hyundai from the previous dream was closest.

It's the car I always drive, pretty much from when I started this job
which was pretty much after my tour ended---
This means I got home…
It's only a dream, don't be stupid.
"Come on, Killer, I need you to focus---"
Brad, the boss: Tall. Blonde. A little stooped. Cheap tweed suit.
"Yeah, I was listening…"
"No, you weren't. Are you getting help for your PTSDs or whatever
the fuck you have?"
"No...it's not a problem, really. You told me I am going to pick up
three people---"
"Fuck the people. The most important thing is the box. It is on the
front seat next to you If anything happens to it, you're worse than
fired. You understand what that means, right?"
"Yeah---"
"Army training or not, there are people who can handle that."
"I got it."
Brad just stared at her. He was trying to be a hard ass but she could
tell by the way he moved he hadn't any skills or training.
"Good. If you have to take anyone out protecting the box, you will
be taken care of. Do you understand that?"
"Yeah."
"Is what is in the box any of your business?"
"No."
Brad watched her for a moment. From somewhere in his pants a
phone was beeping.
"You'll be fine."

TWENTY

The flu had her by the next morning. Kelsey didn't feel like showering but also knew someone would be visiting as they had the previous fifteen days. Jerry arrived carrying a tray with a teapot and two cups.

"I thought I would bring you tea this morning. Is that acceptable?"

"Yes, thank you. You brought two cups..."

"Hmmm, well, with everyone getting ill I felt it prudent to have some tea myself. I brought you something else, one moment."

He walked out the front door and came back with something small and black in his hand. A cap: Las Vegas Gamblers. Jerry sat it on the table and looked almost shy. Kelsey was also looking at the cap, hating it for how it made her feel: She *liked* Jerry just as she liked Bud and Lou.

They have you. You let yourself feel that sort of shit and they have you. Can they really buy you with Better Call Saul and a fucking cap?

There were no words, all the conflicting feelings twisted the words and thoughts into a mess.

"Kelsey...we *are* holding you here. Technically, you *are* a prisoner, but we don't want this to be a prison and we are making every attempt to be kind to you."

"And I appreciate that, Jerry, really. You have been kind; aside from that fucked up video of the children burning."

He winced and set down the cup that he had been moving towards his lips.

"That was a bit heavy handed and for that I apologize---"

"It was real, wasn't it?"

"Yes." His voice was so soft it was barely audible.

Jerry composed himself, took a sip of his tea.

"Our group did not blow up your vehicle. We know the people who did. Honestly, we have been fighting them as much as we've been fighting Americans."

"If you don't mean to get information from me or trade me for one of your guys then why am I here?"

"The three of us you have met do not know. I am not being coy, Kelsey; the Commander has not shared his reasons. His orders are to treat you well and give you whatever you please."

"Aside from delivering me back to my people."

Jerry looked up at her, his face soft for once. Under different circumstances she could have found him beautiful.

"Yes, aside from that."

TWENTY-ONE

The flu deepened. Time became even more meaningless. Jerry brought her teas and soups. Days were spent sleeping and with the sleeping came more strange dreams. Kelsey found herself on a desert highway being chased by a semi-truck as the people in the back seat panicked.

Death is nothing to be concerned about; we are safe as long as the box is intact.

And then she was in a large backyard full of children. A beautiful, custom looking cake sat on a table. It was huge, had to be at least nine layers. In contrast the decorations looked cheap as if they had been picked up at a Major Dollar. One little girl was in a wheelchair. She looked happier than the others and that struck Kelsey. Another little girl was wandering around grabbing balloons from where they were hung, pulling them to the lawn, and stomping them. Each time one popped, the sound was tremendous like a gun or a cannon.

"Hey...maybe you shouldn't be popping those."

The girl didn't answer her at first. No, she grabbed another balloon and stomped it---*BANG!*

"It's my fucking party, these are my balloons."

Reach. Unhook. BANG!

"Come on, can't you be nice?"

The little girl stopped what she was doing and stared at Kelsey. She was ten or a hundred or three or a thousand years old.

"You are not in control, you are just a guest here."

And then Kelsey was back in her bed in the bungalow but everything felt wrong and it wasn't just the fever.

The air-conditioner stopped. Come on, guys, I'm sick as fuck and you didn't pay Jihad Power or whatever.

She struggled out of bed. Dust was coming from under the bedroom door. How...

But she knew and when she opened the bedroom door to discover that it had become the front door Kelsey was not surprised. There was nothing out there but rubble and dust and the smell of spent ordinance and---

Death.

Jerry and Bud and Lou...they're all dead.

And for the second time in twenty-one days Kelsey cried helplessly. She hadn't cried when her buddies were blown up and she had to pick one of their feet off her lap---

This is different, this is very different.

She looked up at the camera on the wall. Before there had been a glowing red light below the lens, now the light had dimmed.

TWENTY-TWO

Secure that the camera was not watching her, Kelsey stripped off her underwear and walked naked to the shelf. Exactly one outfit remained. In that moment, still out of sorts with fever and emotions, that detail did not register. It would however be something she would turn over and over in the days that would come.

She dressed and walked out the bedroom door. A man with a rifle was turning on her, Kelsey saw how young and scared he was; she felt the panic coming off him and understood she was about to die---
"She's one of us, dipshit!"A command voice, somewhere out of her line of sight.
The boot lowered his rifle but was still staring at her. Command Voice walked over, a Sergeant. He looked tired and dirty.
"We're here to rescue you, Corporal. We can give you ten minutes to grab your gear."
Kelsey nodded and looked around at the destruction of what had been her living room. The 7-Up bottle lay in the dust. It was intact but the flowers were gone. She imagined Bud smiling his usual smile as he put the flowers in the makeshift vase---
"You with us, Corporal?"
"Okay...yeah."
There was no gear to grab but she needed a moment, shutting the bedroom and staring at the flat screen which had fallen off the wall and cracked.
"I hope you guys didn't suffer. I hope it was quick."
She looked over at the shelf. It wasn't empty, after all; the Las Vegas Gamblers cap was there. Kelsey thought of how beautiful Jerry had been, how awkwardly formal Lou had acted---
She heard the laughter of her friends one last time as she spotted the boy with the phone.
Placing the cap on her head, she walked out of the bedroom one last time.

Part Three:
An Unkindness

ONE

It had to be the most beautiful place in the world: A tropical rain forest ending at glittering white sand where a turquoise sea brought in gentle waves. The woman had the deck of the yacht to herself. The solitude was only broken by a man in a white jacket who would appear every few minutes to see if she needed anything. It would have been the ideal vacation if not for one thing: She wasn't on vacation. In another part of the ship a decision was being made, the decision was whether they would take her down the dock and back to the city or if they would motor out to deeper waters in order to kill her and throw her body into the sea. As bad as that second possibility was it wasn't a given.

It was nearly twilight; surely if they planned to go out into open waters they would have done it while there was still plenty of light. Yes, this was just intimidation--before she knew it the car would be pulling up to the dock to take her back to her hotel suite in the city... Hearing the anchor chain being pulled up and the motor coming to life she closed her eyes and put her hands on the armrests.

The ship crested a large wave. Her eyes were open and there were new angles to the horizon.
I used to think about getting a sailboat...
Where had she heard that? She could see the face of the person who said it: Stocky. Hispanic. Thirty-something--where had the face said that? A party? No, she didn't go to parties; too many people standing around and blocking passages. The office? Possibly---
She closed her eyes again. Thinking about the office led to thinking about another city which led to thinking about the apartment she had shared with someone, someone she had left behind with no explanation. Was he still stuck there with feelings of abandonment or had he moved on? Had she? She searched her mind for feelings of hurt or loss or *anything* and was bothered that there was nothing to find.

I used to think about getting a sailboat…
She remembered smiling politely as the man shared his dream of
getting a boat and just sailing, just living off the ocean.
That would never work, that thought just beneath the polite smile
and nod she had given the man. Had she added "That'd be nice" out
of obligation? Probably.
No, it wasn't a party, they were standing on a pier of all places.
Before she could recall why she had been on the pier that memory
was intercut with another, someone telling her that he loved her---
The man she had shared an apartment with.
And then she was looking across a couch at him. No, it was a car
seat, a back seat---
She had responded by telling him that she loved him as well.
Had she loved him? She was unsure but it had felt like the right
response like nodding and smiling when the man told her about his
dream to *just sail*---
*We could go somewhere, you and me. We're already on our way---do
you see it, too? It's beautiful out there over the horizon or down that
road without a sign. You want to go?*
And she had smiled politely and nodded while thinking *that will
never work*.
How would things have gone if she hadn't told him she loved him?
Unknown.
The man in the white jacket was approaching. She hastily wiped a
line of tears away and pulled a mask back on.

TWO

A few hours earlier she had been sitting on the edge of a bed in a hotel suite.

Everything had been perfect: The thickness of the sheets. The tile in the bathroom. The flower arrangement in a deep green vase. The two foot thick walls keeping out the noise of the vast city that surrounded the hotel.

It was one of the finest hotels in the world but she might as well have been in a Super 8; her mind was elsewhere, off in the midst of her troubles. The woman kept staring at her wheelchair. Like the appointments in the room it was the best money could buy: Lightweight yet sturdy. Ergonomic seat---

It was still a wheelchair.

Her father had suggested that she travel to the city and stay in the hotel---

No, he had *ordered* it.

Her father had been angry, some of it had been new anger and some had been there a long time: The anger at feeling powerless. The anger at feeling betrayed where you can't get revenge or justice because you love the person who betrayed you. He had ordered her to leave for the city but attempted to soften the blow by paying for the hotel suite with the high thread count sheets and artisan tile in the bathroom. It was a beautiful hotel room, the kind most people only get to experience in movies or the pages of glossy magazines---

It was still a prison.

THREE

The sun was over the horizon out but the temperature was still in the 90s. The man in the white jacket appeared every fifteen minutes to ask if she needed anything and each time she said "no." She was treated like an honored guest and would be up until the end.

The ship turned starboard to crest a wave giving the guest a clear view of the beach growing smaller. Land, the last time she'd see it; the shape of hills and docks and buildings growing vaguer as fewer birds circled and called overhead. Looking at the beach a memory came back of running alongside the sea; the only memory she had of using her legs. She could see her friends, see the world jogged up and down as she ran, but couldn't remember how it felt. It seemed a fitting memory as it had taken place days before the chain of events that would lead her to a chair on a ship heading to deeper and deeper water.

FOUR

All signs of land were gone, even the birds. A man had come on deck: Scar on his face. Older than the others. Seeing him made the finality of her situation real, not just educated speculation: That man had a gun under his coat. At some point he would pull it out and shoot her. When he shot the woman in the chair her life would end. *After he shoots me, they will release the brakes on my chair, open that small white gate, and roll me off the edge of the deck and into the sea.*

The worst part was not the idea of death, that didn't frighten her-- What frightened her was being found by the things that lived in the deep sea and they *were* things, not animals---things that were blobs with teeth and tentacles---and they would tear her body apart and consume it.

These feelings, this growing terror, this is what they want.

She was determined not to give it to them. The woman in the chair focused on taking shallow, measured breaths not unlike the ones she took when lining up a shot.

Think about the girl on the beach--where did she go after that?

The next memory in sequence was being in a hospital; a memory of pain, of a doctor explaining to her in accented English that she would never walk again because her spinal cord was too damaged to repair. The way he struggled with the word *damaged* disgusted her; surely a man who couldn't speak was not the best doctor. When her father had come to visit the girl had shared her observations.

Can't we get another doctor? A better doctor could find a way to fix it.

Father had stood there looking at her. He had brought an expensive looking bouquet of flowers and was shifting it from hand to hand as if it were a heavy grocery bag. Father had never been gentle with her and it was clear that he wasn't going to start just because she was in a hospital bed.

He is the best here. Do you think I wouldn't get the best for you?

Here? Why can't I be in the hospital back home?

101

You know why.

And there had been no further discussion about switching doctors.

You know why.

With those three words his voice had lost all compassion, not that there was much to begin with.

Sometime after the flowers had been put in a crystal vase near her bed she had felt a tingle in her right foot.

My foot! I can feel it! Call the doctor!

She must have been happy; the woman could recall the hope and joy the younger version of her had felt but the girl may as well have been a different person because the feelings were lost to her. The doctor had just looked at her sadly before glancing over at her father with fear. Was he scared there would be revenge for not being able to make her walk again? For consigning this powerful man's daughter to urinating and defecating in bags? She had still been a virgin then---would she ever be able to enjoy intercourse with a man? That thought had embarrassed her and she had never asked the doctor nor had she researched it on-line out of fear of what she would learn. That memory led to a recollection of the last apartment she had shared with someone and the last man who would ever tell her that he loved her.

I love you, Jane.

He had said that as he helped her after she slipped in the shower. The man had wrapped a towel around her and said those three words. He looked awkward, sweet; just a harmless man who didn't really know her at all. His eyes turned to her expectantly so she had told him that she loved him as well; not, *I love you, too* but *I love you, as well*. Formal words for situations where we feel out of place. Formal...understanding our role in a situation and the lines we are supposed to recite because the situation is a pantomime to us, not real. Why couldn't she love him? Why couldn't she feel passion and excitement? It would have been such a good thing if she had been able to. Instead, she had left him while he was at work, catching a cab and feeling nothing but worry for her own sake, that she would never feel the elation and warmth and hope of love ever again.

FIVE

Was the ship slowing? Had the man come closer or was it her imagination?

Would he shoot her with no witnesses or would the Boss come up on deck? When the man with the scar shot her would she just slump or would the force knock her out of her chair?

There was no answer to any of her questions.

All that was certain was that they would toss her weighted body into the water because that was the way it was done.

And she would sink, hundreds or maybe even thousands of feet--

And the things would smell blood and glide through the water as their horrible mouths opened into hungry smiles…

Not helping. Not helping at all.

Jane closed her eyes and went back to the apartment, to the man wrapping a towel around her and telling her that he loved her.

Not much better.

She heard the sound of shoe heels on a metal ladder and turned to see a man coming on deck. He had styled gray hair, tanned skin, and a tailored jacket around his shoulders like a cape. The Boss's eyes were hidden by designer sunglasses. Seeing Jane looking over at him he smiled and nodded politely. The Boss came up behind her and crouched down close enough that she could smell the coffee and teak of his cologne. He released the brake on her chair and rose to full height to push her over to the rail. The gate was an arm's length away. It looked flimsy, surely not sturdy enough to stop her if the ship lurched or was tilted by a wave. She replayed the moment when she had blown the top of a man's head off, the Boss's nephew. Was he imagining what it had looked like as he pushed her chair closer to the edge of the deck?

"Have they gotten you everything you wanted?"

His tone was civil. There was no need for rudeness, it was too late for that. It had been too late when the men had shown up at her beautiful hotel suite.

"Yes, thank you."

He leaned against the railing and Jane wondered what he saw. How many other *guests* had been brought out to that very spot?

"You do very good work, we have admired it for some time now." She looked over at him, he was smiling. Jane nodded her gratitude at his compliment. She had murdered his nephew and now he was having her killed. They were all professionals, there were rules and codes and a certain civility to all the bloodshed and violence. The Boss looked over his shoulder and nodded at the man with the scar who began walking over. His jacket was unbuttoned, revealing a gun that had only been alluded to before. Walther PPK. A civilized gun for a civilized execution on a beautiful boat.

"I'm sure we'll see each other again," the Boss said.

The distant sound of the engine ceased, they were drifting.

"Yes, that's how these things usually work," she replied.

The Boss stepped away and took his sunglasses off. Jane looked out at the sea, watching a wave grow taller in the distance. Under the sound of the water she heard the sound of shoes taking two steps forward, the minute sound of metal on leather, a familiar click---

I love you...as well.

Don't we all die wishing we could have changed at least one thing?

Change--what I said or who I am and what I feel or don't feel?

The wave kept growing and coming closer, she got the feeling that it was going to eat the ship---

There was an explosion with no end; pain never came but there was the sensation of falling forward.

SIX

It came: The vomit, all over her desk; at least she had the sense to shove her tablet aside. How long had she been asleep? No, how long had she been *passed out*? Sitting up was difficult. Holding up the wastebasket to attempt and sweep the vomit into it more so. Cringing, she used her sweater to sweep off the rest of it. The sick girl rummaged in her purse for a mirror---

There was a wheelchair parked off to her right.

Wait.

A wheelchair---

She tried to stand. Her arms and shoulders were ready to cooperate... Everything else? No.

What. The. Fuck?

She had memories of walking through the office building, of seeing all her co-workers and the cubicles from five and a half feet off the ground.

I'm sick, I need to get home and figure this out. This is no place for a panic attack.

She used her tablet to arrange for a ride. The domain for the service was in her memory but when the website asked for a destination address she faltered; what was it? She looked at her purse, ready to rummage for an ID---

No, come on, I have to remember where I live.

She closed her eyes and willed herself to picture the house or the complex---

Nothing.

Defeated, the woman with no memory felt around in her purse until she found her wallet.

Looking over at the wheelchair made her anxious. A car was coming in fifteen minutes, she *had* to climb into it.

There is no reason to panic, I am obviously really sick and forgetting shit...like the fact that I am a paraplegic.

Using her arms she wheeled the office chair over until she was next to the wheelchair.

Obviously I have a system. Everything is going to be okay, this is just some insane flu or whatever it is.

But the weakness was dissipating as was the feverishness and nausea. She put her hand on the wheelchair, the feel of it was familiar, comforting.

I feel better because I just puked, puking is always a relief. The symptoms will come back.

"Feel better, Jamie!"

Someone yelled that as she wheeled down the corridor, watching the world roll by four feet from the floor---why had she remembered *walking*? Clearly she had not *walked* into her office before getting sick. Jamie could feel the heat coming through the entrance doors from twenty feet away, it felt immense.

Am I really going out there? Has it always been this hot?

She rolled up to the doors, reaching out to push the metal bar across one of them. Someone was coming up behind her. Reflexes coming to life, reaching in her bag even if she wasn't sure what for.

"You don't want to do that."

An older man with a mustache and security guard uniform was smiling at her.

"That bar will burn your hand; here, I'll hit the button for you."

He reached over and tapped a blue button which opened the doors. Heat and light rushed in. The guard winced, his hand hovering over the button to close the door after Jamie had passed through.

Am I really going out there?

Understanding there was no choice she rolled through the doors. They immediately closed behind her.

SEVEN

Has it always been this hot?
The woman in the chair felt herself swooning for a moment before something took control of her body: Instinct, the same thing that had caused her to reach in her bag when the guard approached. She scanned the parking lot and then the surrounding rooftops; the woman in the chair had no idea *why* she was doing it just that she *needed* to do it and had always done it.
Something was watching her, something close. Taking a second sweep of her surroundings Jaime saw that there were ravens in the trees, scores of them.
An unkindness. A group of ravens is called an unkindness.
One croaked nearby. Jamie was close enough to see its face as it tilted its head to study her.
"An unkindness. Not really fair is it, Mr. Raven."
There was a single tree over a handicapped space. She rolled over to take advantage of its shade. A couple of hundred feet away people were standing around a bus stop. It reminded her of a story:
A little boy waiting for a bus with a large bottle of water. A little girl stabbed him for it.
Where had that come from? Had someone told it to her or had she actually seen it? Unknown.

A silver SUV pulled into the parking lot that Jamie deduced was her ride. Something about the car turned her stomach, pumped air into her anxiety until it began rising. She imagined a tough looking woman with a Las Vegas Gambler's hat behind the wheel but the man who climbed out was Middle Eastern and older. He was kind and apologetic, hovering as she loaded herself into the backseat. The driver was wearing a shirt that said "Proud American." It made Jamie sad: *He has probably been hassled for his appearance and feels the need to wear a shirt like that just as he felt obligated to stick that little American flag on his antenna.*

He opened a back door. Jamie hoisted herself out of the wheelchair and into the car.

"You must be very strong, you made it look easy."

She was. Jamie had expected it to be difficult climbing in the car but muscle memory and accompanying muscles had kicked in. She touched an upper arm; it was big and solid. The driver went to the back to load her chair in. He struggled to get the hatch open---

That's because this car was rear ended...

It was a ridiculous thought that came out of nowhere but---

In her mind she could see it, a semi rear-ending the Hyundai; it was as if she were watching from the next lane.

She faced forward after getting her seatbelt on. A handful of ravens were circling low over the parking lot.

An unkindness.

EIGHT

The driver was listening to the news: The high that day was supposed to be 126. Another big chunk had broken off of Antarctica. The President was thinking of extending the War to another country. Jamie put her hand on the window; it was too hot to keep her hand on for long.

"You stay in while I set your chair up, it is very hot."

It was. The dash claimed it was 122 degrees outside. Peering around the headrest Jamie saw that the engine temperature was at the three-quarters mark. Her door opened, the driver was standing there smiling. Jamie lifted herself into the chair as the driver held the handles.

"Amazing, it was like watching a gymnast."

She smiled back, it felt good to smile.

The woman in the chair had been delivered to the front door of a large, beige building not unlike the one she had been picked up at. Jamie felt apprehension when she saw a keypad next to the entrance but the numbers came to her without difficulty.

Maybe her memory was coming back---*just a temporary thing, nothing to worry about.* Her condo was on the third of four floors. It was a studio, maybe twenty feet deep by ten wide. Jamie peeked in the bathroom after closing the front door. Something about the bars around the toilet erased whatever happiness she felt; the bars made her being handicapped even more real, permanent.

What is this? If I can move myself around like a "gymnast" then obviously I've been this way for awhile---why am I feeling all this anxiety?

It had to be the sickness messing with her head. There was something else, though, something about the condo didn't feel right.

It feels like a movie set.

Okay, thoughts like that=definitely not helping.

Jamie made tea in her galley kitchen. The condo was tastefully boring: Grays and beiges like the decor of a hotel. Comforts for people just passing through. There was a small desk, wardrobe, dresser, couch, flatscreen on one wall, and a murphy bed she had left pulled down. It had been left in sleep mode but was neatly made. *Professionally made.*

Jamie rolled around the bed studying it; the symmetry was perfect. Could she have done that feeling the way she felt? Could she have done that from a wheelchair?

This is ridiculous. I am being ridiculous.

Am I?

There were croaks off in the distance. Jamie rolled over to the window and pulled the drapes apart enough to see the outside world. Ravens were circling despite the heat. An unkindness.

NINE

A knock on the door was followed a few seconds later by the sound of a key in the deadbolt. She was confused for a moment before remembering who was using the spare key.

"Yeah, sure, come on in...Dad."

Jamie sat up in bed and verified her pajamas were buttoned. Father walked in carrying a container. He was shifting it from hand to hand as if it were hot, making small sounds, playful hoots of pain. Father caught Jamie watching him and smiled over at her.

"I brought you some soup."

"Thanks, just set it on the counter."

"You want some now?" He was bowing a bit, appeared eager to please.

"Nah, just drinking tea right now."

He set the container on the counter and walked over to sit on a corner of the bed. She could smell his cologne, something cheap from a drugstore. His smell was *wrong*; she couldn't explain that intuition but it was undeniable.

Her phone beeped on the nightstand.

I am being ridiculous

"They told me that you left early because you are sick. How are you feeling?"

"Just in that weird flu-like mindspace."

Father leaned over to pat the shape her knee made under the covers. He moved awkwardly; like his scent the hesitation in his movements seemed wrong.

Come on, pull it together, you're just out of it from the illness.

Was she? Yes...she was aware of symptoms. They were weaker than before, though, hopefully they would be gone the following day.

"I need to get some sleep."

Father smiled and nodded, rising from the corner of the bed.

"You are a good girl, I know you will be fine."

Something about the way he said that made it difficult to smile back.

I just need to get some sleep.

Father let himself out. Jamie pulled the covers over her head after hearing him re-lock the deadbolt.

TEN

She was in a shower, had slipped and was sprawled on the pebbled floor of the stall. Someone was holding her and then helping her back onto the seat. A man, somewhere in his thirties, not ugly but not handsome---just a man. White. The only thing that stood out were his golden eyes. Gold like amber.

"I love you," he said.

The water was coming down on both of them but the man seemed unaware of it. Jamie looked at him understanding that he deserved some sort of response.

"I love you, as well."

He smiled at that but there was some hurt in his eyes.

"As well"--what kind of an answer was that?

The man left her to the rest of her shower after helping her back into the chair. Jamie watched him close the curtain and heard the rings jingling.

It is the sort of answer you give someone when you are not sure but feel the need to say something.

She just sat there, the water running over her. It was losing its warmth.

"Ten gallons! Ten gallons! Half of the daily water allotment has been used!"

The harsh, robotic voice shattered the dream and revealed the present.

ELEVEN

The next morning the sickness was gone. Jamie started the coffee and went to take a shower. Pulling the curtains back, the rings connecting them to the shower rod jingled and the music they made brought back the previous night's dream.

She hoisted herself onto the seat but didn't turn the water on.

Jaime *knew* him, he wasn't just a character in a dream, he was *real*. The woman in the shower understood that but her intuitions were also telling her that unlocking his identity was…

Dangerous? The key to finding out everything she was forgetting?

Yes.

The coffee was waiting when she rolled out of the shower. Her phone beeped---

Four months. I've been at that office four months since Amazon delivered me there.

But what did she do? She had an office and not a cubicle so she was probably a manager.

Working for Corporate, not that office, dropped in to…

That was still a blank.

It was nearly a hundred when Jamie wheeled out to the curb. The ravens were circling in the sky calling out or hopping through the grass looking for things to eat. The same gray Hyundai pulled up driven by the same older Arab man. He was wearing a t-shirt with a picture of the President on it and the caption "Booster Boss!"

"Good morning!" the driver called.

Jamie couldn't help but smile back at him and was still smiling as she buckled herself in. The two of them exchanged small talk as he drove: The weather. The latest celebrity scandal. Somehow the conversation veered to something called Simureal.

"…ah, my nephew…he is down at that arcade every couple of days, spends so much money," the driver tsked and shook his head.

"Simureal…I'm sorry, that's something I'm not familiar with."

"Well, as my nephew explained it to me, they can make it so you can have whatever dream you want to have. He tells us he is climbing mountains or flying planes but he is probably doing naughty things." The driver tsked again and then beeped the horn when a car cut him off.

You can have whatever dream you want to have.

Jamie thought of how her bed had looked the previous day, how perfectly it had been made. Not a single wrinkle.

TWELVE

The vomit smell had been cleared out of her office. Jamie pulled the tablet from her bag and set it in front of her. What was she supposed to be doing? What was she in charge of? Still unknown. She squared the sides of the tablet with the sides of the desk. The uniformity was pleasing but didn't help.

Her phone beeped again, maybe it was an update on MeMeMe or something---

Meeting, I have a meeting in fifteen minutes. Bringing the team into the loop on the daily jargon and latest goals.

That was why she had been delivered to the office: That branch's numbers were not optimal. Her job was to pull the team into meetings every couple of hours to revisit their individual numbers with respect to corporate standards and drill them on the new jargon and---

Jamie saw the man in the shower again. He had a few days beard growth.

He has delicate skin, can't shave every day.

Another detail like the smell of the drain backing up in the shower.

This memory is part of something….

But what was that? Was it benign or had she forgotten it on purpose? Would probing deeper into the memory be like taking a submarine deep into the sea where danger waited? Danger in the form of dark smooth things with harsh mouths ringed with teeth.

Jamie murdered the ten minutes before the meeting by bringing up the site for the Simureal arcade and starting a conversation with a CSR. The avatar was an attractive Chinese woman somewhere in her mid-twenties with a big smile.

"Hello, Jaime! What dreams can we make come true for you?"

"I've heard you can give me whatever dream I want."

The avatar's smile got even larger and happier, a predator smelling blood.

"Yes! Would you like me to book an appointment? We have a limited time offer of one free session if you sign on for five sessions at the regular rate."

"Maybe later. I have a question: Could you implant memories in someone?"

The smile faltered on the avatar, became tighter, forced.

"We have a limited time offer of one free session if you sign on for five sessions at the regular rate. Would you like to sign up now?"

"What about implanting memories?"

"I'm sorry, I didn't understand you. Can you---"

The avatar disappeared and the site was replaced with a news feed: The day's viral video was Liam Gallangher's dentures popping out during a concert---

"Oh, now your memories have fucking teeth!" The singer had shouted.

Jamie's phone beeped again, it was time for the meeting.

THIRTEEN

Rolling to the meeting, Jamie struggled to remember what she was supposed to talk about. Passing a cubicle that smelled like coffee spilled on fabric her phone beeped to let her know that it was going to be a degree cooler than the previous day. She looked at the cartoon sun on her phone screen and all the words and topics of the meeting were back in her head. It was a relief but it also made her uncomfortable. She rolled on; you don't curse angels after they save your life.

The only glitch in the meeting had been when an intern shared a rumor she'd heard that the President was dead and his appearances were a hologram owned by Disney. The room fell silent, everyone looked a combination of angry and scared. Had the lights dimmed or was it imagination? Jamie played the rumor off and got the meeting back on track. She kept looking over at the intern, though; the young woman's eyes were fearful.

Her father had left a message while she had been conducting the meeting. She rang him back. He answered on video while walking through a shitty looking store---
The Major Dollar he manages.
---asking her to hold on while he walked to his small office. The screen froze on his picture for nearly a minute: Father's smiling face. The shot had been taken by her mother in the backyard after a barbeque. It had been a good day, a few years ago, before it got really hot. It was a good memory but it felt pasted on, a fake picture in a stolen passport. Father came back in real time. Jaime pushed her concerns down as far as they would go and even managed a small smile.
"Sorry about that, kiddo. Busy day. Coolers going out again."
Father was standing in an alcove with a plastic curtain that served as his office. The curtain was gold colored and had black boats on it.

119

There was a picture on a shelf: Man, woman, two small children, all white and blonde.

"You should tell them to buy new ones," Jaime suggested.

Father laughed too big and bright. It reminded her of the way he had patted her knee, not attached to anything real.

"Ah, that would be a big black mark against me! Boss man doesn't like spending money!" He looked relieved to have an excuse to smile less. Father turned his phone, making it so she could no longer see the family picture.

"Tell me, how are you? Did you eat the soup?"

"Better. No...I just slept after you left, didn't wake up until my alarm."

Father licked his lips as he stared into the corner of the phone with the camera. He seemed to be blinking a lot.

"Do you remember how I lost the use of my legs, father?"

The smile left his face entirely. She could see him trying to remember---

Not a memory. This reminds me of the intern...the scared one when I was coaching her on the daily jargon. Angela.

"Why do we have to talk about that?" Father sighed.

"Do you---"

"Of course!" He was looking down as if his memories were written on the floor. "Why are you asking? You are acting very crazy!"

There was fraying at the edge of his voice as it rose; looking back at the camera on his phone and then off to the side.

"I'm sorry. It must be the sickness," she made an apology out of obligation, assembling it in the same place she had come up with *I love you, as well*.

Her father forced himself to look at the camera again.

"I have to go and deal with my store now. Pull yourself together."

FOURTEEN

One of the team had to leave early. They had bought something at the Major Dollar that had given them food poisoning.

Smelled bad, shouldn't have eaten it.

Jamie read their message over and over. It was innocuous, tossed off, but she found herself looking at it every few minutes: They had perceived something was wrong, that they were making a mistake, yet they carried on.

Her own lunch sat in front of her untouched. Jamie hadn't even remembered making it just as she couldn't remember making her bed without a single flaw.

The tablet beeped, a book she had been looking into was on discount at---

I am being ridiculous. Something about that flu or whatever it was has been fucking with my head, that's all.

That thought, large and with clearly printed letters. Her intuition was telling her that the thought was hollow.

If I popped it what would be inside?

Her phone beeped reminding her that she hadn't posted on MeMeMe in a long time.

I've got to stop being stupid, there is too much work to do.

FIFTEEN

"Is your ride here, Jaime?"

The security guard. Smile peeking cautiously from under a white mustache.

"No, I was just going to wait outside for him."

"It's 120 degrees out there, Jaime." Concern and something else.

"It's been a weird couple of days," she replied. "I could use an intense dose of reality."

He just looked at her. His face was so blank it was impossible to predict what he'd say next.

"If you pass out, I ain't going out there." She could tell by his voice that he hoped that threat would jar some sense into her.

He pushed the button and she went through the doors. The heat wrapped around her, weighed on her, entered her nose and mouth and cooked her from the inside out and outside in. Jaime could feel and smell her hair cooking. There was another odor, one that didn't belong; a decay smell, things washed up on a beach. She wheeled over to the only shade in the lot. Over at the bus stop an old guy with dayglo yellow shoes was dancing. Was he dancing or having a seizure from the heat? The gray Hyundai pulled into the lot. A larger American flag had been attached to the antenna, this one big enough to easily cover a dinner plate. She had another flash of a tough blonde behind the wheel, the same one as before with the cheap sunglasses and Las Vegas Gambler's cap.

No, it was Achmed with his kind smile and Booster Boss shirt. He pulled up to the curb and through the glass she could tell that he was upset.

"Why are you out here?" He chided her. "It is way too hot to be sitting out!"

"I just came out, haven't been here long. Does that guy at the bus stop look like he's having a seizure to you?"

He ignored her question, shaking his head and muttering something that she didn't understand. After Jaime climbed in he rolled her chair towards the trunk.

122

"I worry my car will overheat if it continues to be so hot," Achmed said.

Buckling her seat belt, Jamie closed her eyes. She heard him putting her chair in the back as he mumbled something in a language she didn't understand.

The smells changed: Sweat. Baked goods.

There was the sense of motion, not of moving through the parking lot but traveling at freeway speed, the motor protesting as if it had lost overdrive---

No, she was up in a disused building aiming a rifle. She was lying against a ledge, her legs spread out behind her. Jamie could feel them cramping…

"Does the heat make you sleepy? It makes me sleepy sometimes." Achmed was looking at her in the rear view mirror. Jamie opened her eyes and smiled agreeably. She pulled out her phone and re-read the message from the team member who had left early: They had gotten something foul from the Major Dollar. They could tell something was wrong but ate it anyway.

The news was a soundtrack for the journey from office to condo: The President was touting his successes in the War. Some celebrity had a new fashion line or mixtape or book or something. Scientists were struggling to find a means of dealing with the heat that was killing crops all over the world.

Jamie's phone beeped: McBell had a new menu item and thought she'd like to know since she had---

SIXTEEN

Back in her apartment, Jaime drifted from place to place on-line and then made dinner. Re-watching *Better Call Saul* seemed good; she watched five episodes before sleep overcame her.

In her dreams she was on the ledge again, aiming a rifle as her legs cramped. Down the scope, a man in a suit was walking with men who looked like guards. And then the man in the suit's head was exploding and the guards were looking all around.
This is where it all starts.
She rolled back and out of sight of the guards as they looked up.
"You need to remove the evidence, give me the rifle."
A man was standing a few feet behind her. Expensive suit, designer sunglasses, grim look. There was an understanding---in the dream, at the very least---that this man was her father, her *real* father.
Obediently, Jamie handed him the rifle and---
How do I just stand?
"Come on, time is short. Like we trained you."
Her legs did their part in getting her to a standing position. She could feel the weight of her body on them, feel how the cramps made her muscles ache. Father was pushing at her shoulder and not gently. Jaime shook off the wonder of being on her legs and walked through a sliding glass door into a hotel suite. No, it was a small apartment---
The shower was already running. Jamie took off her clothes and when she pushed the curtain open the rings made delicate music.
The cramps in her legs made it painful to stand. She sat on a seat but the seat tilted and she fell off.
I can't feel them anymore, my legs…
This is how it begins.
It was unfair; she had felt them, had been able to stand and walk and now…
They were gone again, taken away a second time.

124

Sprawled under the water, Jaime began to cry. Someone was pulling the curtain aside. Arms were around her, helping her back onto the seat. It was the man---(*Joe, I call him Joe out of habit but that isn't his real name...*).

"You okay?"

She just nodded, too hurt inside and out to form words.

"I love you," Joe said.

Jaime looked at him. She felt fond of him, definitely cared for him; the four words he was expecting should have come naturally and without hesitation---

"I love you...as well."

And then an alarm was sounding followed by a harsh, robotic voice: "Ten gallons! Ten gallons!"

SEVENTEEN

Jamie woke up completely under the covers. The alarm was beeping and she had no idea what day it was: Wednesday? Friday? Was it the weekend and her phone had just gone off automatically? She rolled over, stuck an arm out from the safety of her nest, and when she pulled the arm back in it was grasping the phone. Thursday. Corporate had texted the day's jargon for the first meetings...Thursday.

The predicted high was 124 that day. Jaime started the coffee and wheeled into the bathroom for her shower. She remembered how upset father had become when asked about what had happened to her legs. The phone beeped on the counter, probably something about a sale or a story she had been following or---
An accident. A friend was showing off and lost control of the car, we hit a utility pole. No, my friend was drunk and I lost my way until I discovered cartooning---no, not cartooning, I went to school. Management shit. I eventually got a job with the company I work for...
Her head hurt and everything---
*Is this really my life? Is this really the life I should be leading because it feels **wrong**. Does this life make me happy because it doesn't feel that way.*
She could feel the bumps of the textured plastic seat against her naked skin. The designer probably though giving it texture would keep the user from sliding off or something---
That led to her thinking about her most recent dreams:
I don't think that those were dreams, I think they were memories--Really? When I had the use of my legs? When I was a hitman?
She tried to remember the earliest days of not having use of her lower body; she tried to remember when she was in the hospital recovering.
*Am I forgetting because I was on heavy drugs? Shouldn't something that intense and painful and traumatic be **burned** into my memory?*

126

It wasn't, and it bothered her.

EIGHTEEN

Jamie got through her shower, washing off the previous day's grime and sweat and dead skin.

Only her troubles remained.

What if there wasn't a car accident? What if I really was a hitman and in the course of my occupation I got shot and that's what paralyzed me?

She had to stretch to reach the deoderant. Stretching felt good, there was something real about the way her arm popped and the way her muscles felt when her arm extended. She began exploring her back with her fingers; all she felt was smooth skin, no scar tissue or anything like that. Jamie rolled over to the cabinet and rummaged around until she found a handheld mirror. It was round and four inches in diameter with a black backing.

Do I really want to do this? What if I actually find a scar from a bullet? Maybe this isn't a memory I should be bringing back to the surface.

She stared at herself in the mirror, turned the mirror over and over in her hands.

I need to know. This is going to bug me until I check it out.

The woman in the chair leaned forward and twisted around to see her back while struggling to maneuver the mirror.

NINETEEN

"I think all the meat has spoiled, Mr. Chen. You smell that? That's a bad smell."

A male employee somewhere around twenty was saying that to Jamie's father.

"No, no, it's fine," father said. "It's supposed to smell like that. Excuse me, I need to talk to my daughter. Hold on Jaime, let me get to my office."

Father stared into his phone as he walked; his face looked troubled as it bounced along and went from light to shadow and back to light again.

"I can tell you are troubled," he said to the phone. "I'm sorry I was harsh with you yesterday."

The bouncing face had sweat on the upper lip and drops scattered around the forehead.

Major Dollar doesn't air condition the warehouse. Dad promised his workers he'd change that when he was made manager. When he didn't, one worker quit and called Dad a bunch of names.

"Okay, I am in my office."

He smiled. The fear had left his face; father looked genuinely kind and loving: Why had she doubted him, who he was?

Yeah? Then how do you explain what was in the mirror?

"Father...was I in a car accident when I was seventeen?"

His face changed---was the anger coming back? Maybe not, but there was something on the edges of the kindness and the love.

"Yes, a car accident. Your friend lost control, we were very scared."

Should I really take this any further?

"I looked at my back this morning...with a mirror..."

The love and kindness were gone. There was nothing there, just a sweaty face; it made her think of a computer that had overloaded and crashed.

"He is right, the meat is spoiled." Very soft, barely audible. "Maybe this is good. I am not happy doing this."

"Doing what?"

129

The man reached towards his phone and the screen went blank.

TWENTY

The association had put up a thermometer in the lobby along with a sign over the entrance: *Wait For Your Ride*. There was a bus stop across from the condos but Jaime couldn't remember anyone waiting at it; most people at the complex were well off enough to afford shared rides or even their own cars. More details were coming back. It was not enough to make her feel comfortable in what was supposed to be her life.

The phones are not safe. I will come by your apartment this evening. After being hung up on someone had slipped that note under Jamie's door. She couldn't wait for the visit, she also wanted to bar the door and not let the truth in.

It was half past seven when the silver Hyundai pulled up. The flag hanging from the antenna seemed larger, the size of a pillowcase. The thermometer claimed it was 106 outside. Had it even gotten below 100 the night before?

The driver was wearing a shirt with a picture of the Twin Towers in mid-collapse. Below the grim picture was the caption: "9/11--NEVER FORGET." It seemed an ill-advised shirt for an Arab-American to be wearing. On the news, the President was lashing out at the Disney rumors, reminding Americans of the "fine results from his previous physical" and how his doctor said that he was "a great specimen for being in his eighties." The President then railed about "fake news" and joked about having history professors shot. They pulled into the carpark surrounding Jamie's office. Achmed leaned forward and seemed to be watching the ravens. Next to him the dashboard thermometer claimed it was 109 degrees.

"I saw a terrible thing yesterday," Achmed sighed.

"What was it?" *Do I really want to know?*

"I was driving by a bus stop and a little girl punched a little boy for a bottle of water."

What the driver shared brought on a wave of anxiety for some reason. In her bag the phone beeped to let her know that the store where she had bought her make-up was having a limited time sale. Achmed was watching her in the rear view mirror with a serious expression.

"I am sorry if my story upset you."

"It's okay---"

"That boy should have known better than to flash a big bottle of water at a bus stop; people are very thirsty in this heat."

He smiled in the mirror but it looked forced.

"I will get your chair."

Wheeling into the building, Jaime thought about the meeting and how embarrassed Angela had been.

I need to talk to her, let her know that everything is okay.

She took a detour to the cubicle the intern worked out of. There was a young man and women in there but no Angela. Both interns were working on tablets and checking their phones at the same time. Neither seemed to register the woman in the wheelchair watching them.

"Did they move Angela?"

The girl looked up from her phone. She had bad skin under her makeup.

"Who?"

"Never mind, I'll ask security."

Jaime wheeled around until she found the older man with the mustache. He smiled and asked how she was dealing with the heat. She said she was getting on fine and then asked about Angela. The security guard's smile faltered but he tried to cover it up.

"Ah, Angela. She got transferred to another place, I believe."

"Another place?"

The smile became bigger, clenched looking, giving him three chins.

"That's all I know."

There were three ten minute meetings before lunch to go over the day's jargon. Between meetings, Jaime wheeled to team member cubicles to go over their numbers and take her coaching opportunities and---

A team member was earnestly rattling off ways of improving her customer approach while working in the new jargon while---

Jaime drifted off. Her eyes must have closed because she was no longer in that cubicle, she was in a silver Hyundai but they weren't in the city and Achmed wasn't driving; it was someone with long, blonde hair pulled into a strict ponytail and held down by a cap. Jaime was on someone's lap and they were on a desolate highway, speeding along a downgrade. She reached down for the man's hands, put them on her breasts.

"Are you okay, Jaime?"

"Uh, yeah, just, uhm, listening. I think you're on the right track, maybe you could also…"

Somehow Jaime knew what to say and said it. They weren't her words and ideas, though, it felt like they were simply coming through her independent of her own brain.

Ten minutes later she was back in her small office thinking about the boy being stabbed at the bus stop and the sensation of the man's hands on her breasts.

It's the same man that's in the shower, my boyfriend or whatever he is…was.

Her phone beeped. It was Amazon. She would be delivered to a different office the following Monday.

TWENTY-ONE

The co-worker who had gotten the bad meat from Major Dollar was
back. He was still suffering but unrepentant.

"It was my fault, I should have seen the green on the meat. Normally
that store has been awesome---have you seen the prices?"

Jaime struggled not to smell his spasming bowels. Her phone beeped
to let her know the air had reached 123 degrees in her zip code and
offered the suggestion of carrying lots of water.

Just don't flash it at bus stops.

The man with the mustache was near the door looking out. Had he
been wearing a cap reading *Security* earlier?

"This heat has to end sometime, right?" He said.

She just smiled at him and went through the doors.

Instead of the Hyundai an old looking Mercedes Benz was waiting
at the curb. As she rolled through the office doors a Chinese man in
a designer suit and shades burst from the driver's door and hustled
over to assist her. Jaime recognized him but it took her mind a few
seconds to place him: The roof, it was this man who had taken the
rifle, not father; both of them had been younger then---

What did it mean? How...

Johnny Bahn, that was his name, and he was behind her pushing her
chair to the nearest back door of the Mercedes.

"Yeah, your head is probably spinny spinny right now, J," Bahn said
through a lopsided grin. "It's okay, your father will talk to you about
it."

The air conditioning was weak in the old car. Jaime could feel sweat
forming on her face, a thin mask. So many masks---you pull one off
hoping for a face but it's just a different mask. Her phone beeped.
There was no message but the anxiety that had been building
seemed to have reached a plateau.

At the condo complex Johnny Bahn got her wheelchair out, waited
for her to climb into it, and wheeled her into the lobby. He took in

their surroundings as he smoked a cigarette. A robotic voice like a mechanical smile chimed from somewhere like a steel ghost.

"No smoking, please!"

"You fuck yourself, okay?" Johnny waved.

He took a long drag, sat in a chair across from Jaime.

"You're gonna be okay, Big J. We train you to be strong."

"What's going on, Johnny? My memories are all fucked up."

The man with the cigarette got up from the chair.

"Your father is waiting for you in the condo."

The condo, not *your* condo. Semantics. Sometimes semantics are everything.

TWENTY-TWO

A stranger wearing an expensive suit and a sullen expression was sitting at her kitchen table: Father, her *real* father. Who was the man who had brought her pho and had talked to her through the phone? Would it ever be explained? Did it even matter? Father gestured for her to sit at the table where he had set two tumblers of scotch.

"I take it you can't get that at the Major Dollar," she said.

"What?" His tone was harsh, father was irritated.

"The scotch...never mind."

It had always been that way when she attempted to joke with him. *This is the real father...for better or for worse.*

She sat at the table and savored the smell of the whiskey, swishing it in the glass to admire how it captured the light in the room.

"What did you see on your back?" Father asked.

She took a sip. He could wait after all she had been put through.

"Some red lines and scar tissue over what looked like a hole," Jaime said.

Father took a sip from his glass. Had he always had a gold tooth in front? Would she ever be able to trust her memories again?

"Memory is a place where we burn," those words very quiet as if he were talking to himself.

"Pardon?"

He looked down at the table, began tracing circles with the index finger of his left hand.

"The hole is from the bullet...they operated on you a few times trying to see if they could fix your spinal cord. They couldn't...obviously. It wasn't supposed to be there. You should know that I usually don't miss details."

"What do you mean?"

The finger that had been tracing the circle became part of a fist.

"I invested a lot of money in Simureal; I will be taking it back," he said grimly.

"Invested in the company or the technology?"

136

"Both. I will hold my investment in the tech; it will be huge, but not for a couple more years."

She noticed that two large suitcases were on the kitchen linoleum. Where would she be going? Back to the apartment she had been dreaming of, the one with the shower and the man who told her that he loved her?

"Was the problem with my memories coming back? I'm not even sure which were my real memories," she said.

Father waved off her question, took a drink.

"The problem is that there are glitches in the software."

He paused, rested his hands flat on the table looking defeated.

"I tried to protect you but it isn't working," he looked sad.

"What are you talking about?"

Father took a long drink. Anger was flashing through the defeat.

"I had them bring you here. The idea was to give you a good life, the most important part of you, but this software...I'm sorry."

"I still don't understand."

His tumbler was nearly empty. Where was the bottle? In her cupboard? Had it always been there?

"They tell me that it can be fixed, that the memories will disappear and it will be just a good life with no troubles. I have been promised it will smooth out, become like a very pleasant dream."

Father got up and went to the cupboard. He grabbed the bottle of scotch and then put it back.

"Be strong," he said with a tight smile. "You are strong, things will be okay."

"Are you telling me that I am inside of this thing called Simureal?"

"Yes. You are safe, keep that in mind no matter where you go."

Father patted her shoulder and left the condo.

TWENTY-THREE

It had to be the most beautiful place in the world. Behind her, a tropical rain forest ending at glittering white sand. In front of her, the open sea bringing in gentle waves. The woman had the deck of the yacht all to herself aside from a man in a white jacket who would appear every few minutes to see if she needed anything. It would have been the ideal vacation if not for one thing: She wasn't on vacation. In another part of the ship a decision was being made. The decision was whether they would take her down the dock and back to the city or if they would motor out to deeper waters to kill her and throw her body into the sea. As bad as that second possibility was, it wasn't a given. It was nearly twilight; surely if they planned to go out into open waters they would have done it while there was still plenty of light.

Yes, this was just intimidation; before she knew it the car would be pulling up to the dock to take her back to her hotel suite in the city...
Hearing the chain being pulled up and the motor coming to life she closed her eyes and put her hands on the armrests.

The ship crested a large wave. Her eyes were open and there were new angles to the horizon. Three birds were circling overhead, one called out. They flew out of her line of sight.

I used to think about getting a sailboat.

Where had she heard that? She could see the face of the person who said it: Arab. Male. Somewhere in his sixties. He had been driving her somewhere. She saw him from the back seat so he had to be an Uber driver or something.

I want to say he drove me from work to home and back the next morning.

She closed her eyes again. Thinking about the work led to thinking about another city which led to thinking about the apartment she had shared with someone; someone she had left behind with no explanation. Was he still stuck there in feelings of abandonment or had he moved on? Had she? She searched her mind for feelings of hurt or loss or *anything* and was bothered that there was nothing to find.

I used to think about getting a sailboat.

She remembered smiling politely as the man shared his dream of getting a boat and just sailing, just living off the ocean.

That would never work, that thought just beneath a polite smile and nod. Had she added "That'd be nice" out of obligation? Probably.

No, it wasn't in a hire car, they were standing on a pier of all places. And it wasn't an older Arab, it was a white male somewhere in his thirties---

And then he was telling her that he loved her...

The man she had shared an apartment with.

And then she was looking across a couch at him. No, it was a car seat, a back seat---

She had responded by telling him that she loved him as well. Had she? Maybe not but it felt like the right response like nodding and smiling when the man told her about his dream to *just sail*.

We could go somewhere, you and me. We're already on our way---do you see it, too? It's beautiful out there over the horizon or down that road without a sign. You want to go?

And she had smiled politely and nodded while thinking *that will never work*. The man in the white jacket was approaching. She hastily wiped a line of tears away and pulled a mask back on. Hadn't the man in the white suit been older before? This man was in his forties but hadn't he been elderly before with a white mustache? *This is a fancy boat, I'm sure they have more than one waiter.*

She asked for a tumbler of single malt neat and he was back with it within a couple of minutes. Swishing it, the way it caught the natural light was disappointing; there was too much glare. Jaime took a drink and closed her eyes to escape to another time, another place. A familiar bird call. Looking up she saw three birds circling. Her instincts told her it was the same three birds from before.

The ship turned starboard to crest a wave. The guest had a clear view of the beach growing smaller. Land, the last time she'd see it. The shape of hills and docks and buildings growing vaguer. Looking at the beach a memory came back of running alongside the sea---the only memory she had of using her legs. She could see her friends, see the world jogged up and down as she ran, but couldn't remember how it felt. It seemed a fitting memory for where she was. Right before the start of the chain of events that would lead her to a chair on a ship heading to deeper and deeper water.

All signs of land were gone, even the birds. A man had come on deck: Scar on his face. Older than the others. Seeing him made the finality of her situation real, not just educated speculation: That man had a gun under his coat. At some point he would pull it out and shoot her. When he shot the woman in the chair, her life would end. *After he shoots me, they will release the brakes on my chair, open that small white gate, and roll me off the edge of the deck and into the sea.*
The worst part was not the idea of death, that didn't frighten her--- What frightened her was being found by the things that lived in the deep sea and they *were* things, not animals--things that were blobs with teeth and tentacles...and they would tear her body apart and consume it.
These feelings, this growing terror, this is what they want.

Was the ship slowing? Had the man come closer or was it her imagination?
Would he shoot her with no witnesses or would the Boss come up on deck? When the man with the scar shot her would she just slump or would the force knock her out of her chair? There was no answer to any of her questions. All that was certain was that they would toss her weighted body into the water because that was the way it was done.

140

She would sink, hundreds or maybe even thousands of feet and the things would smell blood and glide through the water, horrible mouths opening in hungry smiles.

Not helping. Not helping at all.

Jane went back to the apartment, to the man wrapping a towel around her and telling her that he loved her---

Is this really any better?

She heard the sound of shoe heels on a metal ladder and turned to see a man coming on deck. He had styled gray hair, tanned skin, and a tailored jacket around his shoulders like a cape. The Boss's eyes were hidden by designer sunglasses. Seeing Jane looking over at him he smiled and nodded politely. The boss came up behind her and knelt down close enough that she could smell the coffee and teak of his cologne. He released the brake on her chair and rose to full height to push her over to the rail. There was a gate an arm's length away. It looked flimsy, surely not able to stop her if the ship lurched or was tilted by a wave. She replayed the moment when she had blown the top of a man's head off, this man's nephew. Was he imagining what it had looked like as he pushed her chair closer to the edge of his boat?

"Did you enjoy the scotch?"

His tone was civil. There was no need for rudeness, it was too late for that. It had been too late when the men had shown up at her beautiful hotel suite.

"Yes, thank you."

He leaned against the railing and Jane wondered what he saw. How many other *guests* had been brought out to that very spot?

How many times have I been here?

"You do very good work, we have admired it for some time now."

She looked over at him, he was smiling. Jane nodded her gratitude at his compliment. She had murdered his nephew and now he was having her killed. They were all professionals, there were rules and codes and a certain civility to all the bloodshed and violence. The Boss looked over his shoulder and nodded at the man with the scar who began walking over. His jacket was unbuttoned, revealing a gun that had only been alluded to before. Walther PPK. A civilized gun for a civilized execution on a luxurious boat.

"I'm sure we'll see each other again," the Boss smiled.

"Yes, that's how these things usually work," she replied.

The Boss stepped away and took his sunglasses off. Jane looked out at the sea, watching a wave grow taller in the distance. Under the sound of the water she heard the sound of shoes taking two steps forward, the minute sound of metal on leather, a familiar click---

I love you...as well.

Don't we all die wishing we could have changed at least one thing?

Change--what I said or who I am and what I feel or don't feel?

What I don't feel, what I cannot feel; I can't be upset for that.

The wave kept growing and coming closer, she got the feeling it was going to eat the ship. There was an explosion with no end; pain never came but there was the sensation of falling forward.

TWENTY-FOUR

A hard blow to the back of the head, darkness, water---
And then hands on her; hands attached to arms helping her onto some sort of textured seat.
The shower. Jaime had slipped off the seat and hit the back of her head.
This will teach me to drink like that; Joe doesn't look much better.
"Shit---you okay?" He looked scared.
"Yeah, just give me a second."
She realized that she didn't want his hands on her. His touch---
In the beginning it had felt right, even excited her, but now---
Why can't I fall for him? Why can't I genuinely lose myself in what we have?
He was watching her closely, probably expecting words.
"So...can we make a deal not to drink like that ever again?" She asked.
The words clearly made him happy. Maybe he had been sensing she was about to break up with him and her statement gave him hope.
"Of course," he smiled.
Why were we drinking like that?
The diagnosis three weeks ago: Funny celebrating over finding a tapeworm egg in someone's head.
A memory: Holding a glass of neat whiskey up and proclaiming "Here's to Tapey!"
And the two of them had laughed and the merriment had continued.
"I love you," he said.
Jaime looked up at him. The shower was still running but the water was nearly cold. Joe didn't seem to notice, he looked earnest, full of expectation--
"I love you...as well." Words, just rolling out, lighter than air.
He looked disappointed by that and stood up to leave the shower.
As well---it just hung there, neither knowing why it felt wrong just that it did. Joe made the shower rings jingle as he left her alone,

subtle music for a dark mood. Jaime sat on the textured plastic seat naked.

"Water usage warning, water usage warning!"

The robot that ran the house yelled that, the robot that ran the world. The water had become cold but she didn't notice. Her response had disappointed both of them and now it was clear where they were at in their life together and what needed to be done. Jaime shut the water off. She didn't want to leave the shower; walking out meant facing him and facing what needed to be said if she was ever to move into the future and create new memories.

Part Four:
Anyone Out Here?

ONE

Dead of thirst surrounded by water.

He stood in the bow and looked out at a view that hadn't changed in weeks: The sea, sometimes angry but calm in that moment. Why did *he* feel so calm? There was no reason to feel tranquil: Unless the desalinator could be fixed they'd be dead within a week. The others were running around and arguing amongst themselves. He was the Captain; it was his responsibility to maintain order, to motivate the crew.

I'm in charge.

It was a weird thought, one that made him uncomfortable. Some people are born to lead but he wasn't one of them. It was easier to just stay in his own head, staring out at the sea, wondering what it was like to die of thirst. They kept looking over in his general direction--*was* there a leader inside him? He had given orders but they had always been casual like suggestions that his crew would hopefully go along with. Maybe the t-shirt and flip flops were part of the problem: Too casual. Too loose. Maybe that's why captains wore the serious jackets and boots in the old days; serious clothes that demand the man wearing them be taken seriously.

We'll be dead of thirst in a week.

That was a serious thought. He looked over at his crew.

Come on, their lives are in my hands, they need me to be a real captain.

"Hey!" Why had his voice cracked? That was hardly helping with the authority issue.

"Hey!" Better. Now most of them were looking over.

"Listen up!" One of the girls got everyone's attention. Show off.

"The desalinator is our highest priority," the Captain said. "Anyone wanna take a stab at it?"

The girl with the authoritative voice winced. The Captain understood his mistake and winced himself.

"Look...everything is okay. I'll get it working. While I am doing that I need Josie and Cameron to figure out a new route, one that takes us out of the doldrums. I need you guys to track the weather and see if you can find us some wind."

That felt good: His voice had been firm and he had given instructions despite the t-shirt and flip-flops.

Now all I have to do is make the desalinator run again.

The captain made his way below-deck. In the open there had been a breeze, not enough to move the ship but sufficient to make the heat bearable. In the hull it was still and hot and smelled like bodies and all the living those bodies did. Kids: Always eating or fucking or smoking marijuana. Even with the breeze it was in the mid-90s out there. In the hull? Enough to make his skin glisten with sweat after a couple of minutes. Sweat, not perspiration. His eyes stung and he blinked helplessly. Deep in the hull there weren't any gorgeous views or the feel of the ocean air on one's skin, it was as dank and dark as a prison. This was not what he had planned when he had bought the boat: Desperate work with wires. The flashlight making his mouth sore as he clamped it in his teeth. Trying to make sense of diagrams and technical jargon.

This hadn't been part of his plan.

There was the problem right there, that word---*plan*. That word had never played a role in his buying a boat, finding the crew, and taking to the open sea; it had been a *dream* or maybe an *ideal*. Plans are constructed out of logic and research with fail-safes and back-up plans waiting in the wings like understudies. Dreams and Ideals are not so solidly built, they just exist out there. Floating; drifting uselessly like a boat on a still sea.

His mouth cramped and it felt like the metal of the flashlight was digging into his fillings. Sweat ran down his back, down the crack of his ass, and soaked his shorts.

We'll be dead with in a week if I don't fix this fucking thing.

A mechanic...a real plan would have included hiring a real mechanic, someone who knows all the sorts of wrenches and other mechanical tools.

The more time he spent down there the more it felt like a tomb.
There was no sensation of movement, the boat wasn't even bobbing.
The others had to be on deck because he couldn't hear any voices.
Was he alone? Was he even on a boat?
"Come on, *focus*."
The words made the flashlight move and scrape a tooth with a
cavity. The pain brought him back; he could think, he could look at
the diagrams and then at the machine and things were starting to
make sense. The filter was clogged: Salt, loads of salt, and a single
bottle cap. He took the flashlight from his mouth and pinched the
bottle cap with his free hand.
Plastic, so much fucking plastic in the ocean.
That was the easy answer; there was loads of plastic in the ocean
choking fish, everyone was aware of it....
But something about that bottle cap bothered him; he had no idea
why but it did.

TWO

The Captain was the only one with a private berth. Sometimes he was grateful for his own space but often it felt lonely. Many nights he'd sit on the edge of the bed listening as they laughed or talked or had sex. The crew all shared one room but sometimes a couple would hook up out there and the sound of fucking would mix in with the conversations and laughter. The kids didn't seem to have any sort of boundaries. Jealousies came up, some lingered and some went away; dynamics shifted and changed like the winds that controlled the boat. The night after he fixed the desalinator it was quiet out there.

Once again the Captain got the undeniable feeling that he was alone. He got up to open the door, felt ridiculous, and sat back on his bed. *I need water. I am not going out there because I am going crazy and think I am alone, I just need water.*
Opening the door he saw the kids were still out there but they seemed subdued. After a few seconds he picked up on other things: Fear. Confusion.
Josie looked over at him and he saw fear on her face. Normally Josie was tough and organized, not one to show weakness. This couldn't be good.
"Jacob is gone," she said, a slight tremble to her voice.
"What? Did he fall overboard? Why aren't we searching for him? Come on, we've got to---"
Josie shaking her head silenced him. She walked to the step ladder that led to the deck and the Captain followed. It was nearly dawn. There was a smell out there that he refused to acknowledge until he saw the blood on the fiberglass. On the edge of the blood was a pair of shorts, Jacob's shorts.
"What the fuck?" The captain asked. "Where is he? Where is the body?"
All that blood and those shorts...and he had his back to the hatch. Any of the kids could sneak up or Josie could pull a knife and---

149

"We don't know, Jorge."

She had put a hand on his shoulder. He didn't mind, in fact he liked it; why couldn't the hand have been there under different circumstances?

"What happened?" Jorge asked.

"We don't know. He had to piss so he went up. He was up here for a while so we thought he was just looking at the stars or enjoying the air or whatever. After a while Cameron had to piss and discovered the blood and the shorts."

"Okay...not to accuse anyone but---"

"Cameron didn't kill him, he didn't have any blood on him."

Jorge wanted to ask more questions but knew there wouldn't be any answers. Why hadn't Cameron yelled? Cameron was the sort of person who would have yelled on finding all that blood---normally. *Unless he killed Jacob.*

No, Cameron was not a killer. He was pretty sure of that. Pretty sure. There was nothing that could be done aside from cleaning the blood up and figuring out what they needed to do about their missing ship mate.

THREE

They got some wind that morning; it ruffled the kids' hair as they cleaned Jacob's blood off the deck. A bird circled overhead. Jorge thought it was a raven but it was probably a gull. Josie looked down at Jacob's shorts for a moment before using the handle of the broom to flick them into the sea. Where they had laid was a cluster of bubbles, most of them red.

The kids seemed alright, not scared or sad about Jacob's disappearance and presumed death.
One of them had to have killed him but why are the others so blase? Was it some kind of sacrifice or a ritual?
That would leave him the odd one out and Jorge didn't like that. What was he supposed to do? Calling some sort of law enforcement was not an option; it was the open ocean, about as lawless a place as one could imagine.
The shorts were still bobbing in the water as the ship sailed on. Jorge watched them grow smaller and then disappear. A man had been inside them, a boy really, and the boy was gone. Violently.

Knowing it was up to him, Jorge gathered the kids around him on the deck. They were all young and relatively attractive---had that been why he had chosen them to be his crew? He had never thought about it, perhaps he should have. They were mediocre sailors at best. Their conduct in the first storms off the coast had been a disaster. Clearly some higher power had been looking after them. Jorge thought of the shorts, the bubbles of blood they left behind.
Maybe that higher power got bored with us.
"I'm going to start with a basic question: Does anyone know what happened to Jacob?" Jorge asked.
They just looked at him with similar facial expressions.
*Oh, God, they're a cult. It **was** a ritual murder; it will be my turn next!*
Not helping. Really...not helping.

151

"He...died?"

"Okay, seeing as he's not on the boat and neither of the liferafts are gone that is a safe assumption..." The captain sighed, starting to feel frustrated.

*Look...if you **are** a cult performing rituals, could you just leave me out of it?*

"We're on our own out here, guys," Jorge continued. "If one of you had an argument with him and things got out of hand...let's talk about it, okay?"

The kids looked at one another. Again, no discernable emotions aside from slight confusion.

"One of you is a killer, okay? This is serious, guys."

They looked at Jorge. Josie spoke up.

"What if it was you, Jorge?"

"Pardon?"

"Why couldn't have been you who killed Jacob?" Josie added.

"I had nothing against him," Jorge replied.

"Neither did I---did any of you?" Josie asked her shipmates.

The other kids murmured that they didn't.

"Come on, I know sometimes there are hook-ups and people get jealous---"

"Jealous but...whatever. It's just fucking bro." Cameron, looking annoyed.

"We're getting nowhere," Jorge sighed. "Let's just get on with what we need to do."

The kids murmured, Josie was looking right at Jorge.

"It's going to be okay, Captain."

"I'm sure it will be...aside from the occasional murder."

She looked out at the sea, in the general direction of where Jacob's shorts were still bobbing if they hadn't sank.

"We're all just guests here, we're not in control."

FOUR

Josie managed to catch a large fish. The kids whooped, stripped naked, and rubbed their bodies with its blood and offal. Jorge looked on horrified for a moment and then remembered that the kids always did that, it was a harmless ritual.

Is it?

Part of him was sure it was the first time they'd done it, part of him thought the ritual had occurred in the past--

We hadn't caught a fish in weeks. I want to say Jacob caught one and the others were so excited that they decided to thank the fish or the gods or the fish gods with a ritual dance.

Jorge could see it in his memory…

Or was it his mind playing a trick on him?

That afternoon, the first one without Jacob, he watched the kids stripping and covering themselves with blood and dancing. Jorge contemplated joining them but didn't: He felt older---older and fat. Besides, he was the Captain and had to show some authority. Most importantly, he didn't feel like he was one of them.

He cooked the fish with some rice. The others were still keyed up from the ritual and hadn't bothered washing the blood off. They put their clothes back on when darkness brought a chill but their visible skin was still streaked with blood. The kids were still chatting excitedly when he retired to his berth.

How can they sound so happy when one of them has disappeared? No, how can they sound so happy when one of them was probably brutally murdered?

"It's because they're a fucking cult," Jorge whispered to himself. "I've brought a murder cult onto my fucking boat."

Alone in the darkness he chided himself for his crew selection and realized that he couldn't remember hiring them---had he asked around? Put an ad on Craigslist? Where had he found the kids? Anxiety: Why couldn't he remember?

Calm the fuck down. You're just stressed over Jacob's disappearance and it doesn't help that they're acting like nothing has happened. Is it shock? No, shock hits people differently, they are all acting the same.

Jorge lay in bed, closed his eyes, and focused on his breathing. One of the kids had picked up the acoustic guitar and was playing what sounded like an Oasis song. The Captain found himself in the back of a car speeding through a desert. There were three other people, two women and a man. This was either a memory he couldn't place or he had drifted off and was dreaming---

It felt real, though, felt like something he had experienced and that just added to his anxiety.

FIVE

This time there was hair, a lot of hair.

Bethany is gone.

That morning it had been Cameron knocking on his door. The boy still had specks of dried fish blood on his bare chest. Jorge walked up to the deck. The kids trailed after him and everyone stood in a circle around Bethany's tank top, frayed brown shorts, what was presumably her spattered blood.

And hair, a lot of hair.

No one said anything. The only sound was the sail fluttering weakly and the splash of the ocean on the hull. Jorge looked out at the horizon. He thought that he was looking north but maybe he was turned around. They were a long way from land, easily a thousand miles maybe two.

"So...we're going to stick to the story of no one knowing what happened here?" he asked the kids.

"Do *you* know what happened, Jorge?"

The Captain looked down at the hair. It had probably been ripped out. Had she been alive? No, that would have made her scream. Why hadn't there been any shrieks or cries or the sound of struggle? It must have been quick, one of the arteries in her neck must have been slit or something. Jorge imagined Bethany smiling and laughing as it happened and that image was worse than the blood and all the hair.

"Four more nights."

"Four more nights *what*, Jorge?"

"And then the killer will have no one left to kill."

SIX

The smell of burning plastic was in the cabin: The desalinator; it was eating itself again. Jorge went below-deck, grabbed the instruction manual, and sat cross legged next to the malfunctioning machine. It was difficult to focus when he kept seeing blood on the deck, blood and Bethany's hair...the image of her laughing as her neck was slit open.

Two more nights at most and then I will be murdered on the deck. One of them is a killer, I can't imagine any of them being a brutal murderer but one of them has to be---unless I've been slipping into one hell of a fugue state.

No, his berth opened into the main cabin; the kids would have said something. Jorge stopped what he was doing and studied his hands, looking for any trace of blood. He checked his clothes---nothing.

The past two days he had been working backwards trying to recall where and when he had met his crew. The furthest back he had been able to get was the first ritual of the fish, the girls stipping their clothes off and coating themselves with blood as they laughed. Their bodies were a distraction, he had to concentrate---

He saw a colorful looking bus in a Major Dollar parking lot. Not a full sized bus, one of the short ones. The kids were standing near it. Why were there six of them in the memory? Weren't there only five including the two who had disappeared?

Focus.

A cop SUV was nearby. Were the cops hassling the kids? No, the cops were nowhere to be seen. And then there was the sound of gunshots inside the store. It didn't seem to register with the kids, they were standing around the front of the bus trying to figure out how to make it go again. Why had he brought them on the boat? How had they convinced him they'd be a good crew?

Those memories were lost.

SEVEN

Cameron. Josie. Keith.

One of them was a brutal killer. There was the remote possibility someone on another boat was stalking them but it was extremely remote: There was nowhere to hide with few clouds and a calm sea. It had to be one of the three remaining kids.

Jorge was bigger than any of them, maybe as big as two of them put together, but the killer had insanity on their side. His throat itched, imagining the rasp of a knife somewhere out there destined to break his skin.

Cameron. Josie. Keith.

If that night was like the previous two, one of the kids would be disappearing before the sun rose.

A submarine? One lurking right below the hull?

Ridiculous. Absolutely fucking ridiculous.

Some sort of sea creature sweeping a tentacle across the deck when it sensed fresh meat? Did any of them do that? Jorge was pretty sure they didn't but now had that added to the horrors in his head; something featureless aside from waving tentacles and a mouth full of fangs.

One of the last things you want to think about thousands of miles from land.

There was no sound in the main part of the cabin. Maybe they had gotten to sleep---

Maybe it's two of them working together, killing the rest of us off one by one.

Don't be an idiot, crazy people don't work together.

Maybe they're not crazy. We are running low on food stores and not catching enough fish to sustain us. Maybe I'm still alive because I can keep the desalinator running.

Hadn't one of the kids been shadowing him when he worked on the machine? Watching him closely as if to learn how to mend it?

Which one was it? Why couldn't he see a face?

Cameron. Josie. Keith.
Which one, he had no fucking idea.

EIGHT

Jorge eventually slept. His dreams were, as predicted, horrific. Someone creeping up behind him, slashing his belly open and yanking his guts off as he watched. It hurt---are you supposed to feel pain in dreams? He had wanted to wake up but it had taken forever, looking down at his intestines in wonder and terror: *There's no fixing that.*

Light was coming through his porthole. It was morning, the time when ghouls are supposed to retreat into the mist, but he still didn't want to leave the relative safety of his cabin. He stared at the door and dug around inside until he was able to unearth some strength, Not much, just enough to turn a handle and push a piece of wood on hinges. Cameron and Josie were sitting at the table, two people at a table that could seat up to eight. They were eating oatmeal listlessly and not looking at each other. Josie glanced up when Jorge's door opened. She smiled at him. He saw it as a flirtatious smile and chided himself for a number of reasons.
"Where's Keith?"
Josie stopped smiling and looked down into her bowl.
"He was gone when we woke up…"
"Neither of us have wanted to go on deck," she added. "I mean, it was stuffy in here last night, he could have just gone up to sleep in the fresh air…"
None of them believed that; they looked at each other *knowing* Keith wasn't just hanging out on the deck. Part of him probably was, maybe a couple of pints of blood and possibly some hair but not the Keith they all knew and tolerated. Jorge looked over at the step ladder. Josie and Cameron stood up.
Maybe one or both of them wants to be there when I discover Keith's remains like when you have a cat and it leaves "presents" for you.
He went up the ladder and let his eyes adjust to the morning sun.
The sails were still up.
Careless. They should know better than that…

159

Up near the bow was the blood, a lot of it same as the previous two nights.

"Why do we even bother cleaning it up?" Cameron said in a thoughtful tone of voice.

In the middle of the blood was a foot severed just above the ankle. The three of them walked over and cast shadows on it. One of Josie's toes was in the blood, she didn't seem to notice and that raised Jorge's suspicions even further.

Sea creatures don't neatly remove feet like this. That foot wasn't bitten off, it was sawed off.

"Maybe we should eat it."

Josie. The other two looked over at her. She met their gazes.

"We're running out of food and there aren't many fish…"

Jorge picked up the foot and threw it, the splash in the water was pronounced.

"Isn't that going to draw sharks?" Cameron, again thoughtful.

The Captain shook his head and walked off to get the brush they had used to clean up blood the previous two days.

NINE

Cameron whistled a little as he scrubbed blood off the deck and it caught Jorge's ear. He said nothing to Cameron but filed the whistling away in a large cabinet labeled SUSPICIOUS BEHAVIOR. The Captain went to where Josie had one hand resting on the wheel. She looked so natural; maybe he should make her the captain. Her hair was pulled back in a ponytail and mostly kept secret under a battered Las Vegas Gamblers cap. He stood behind her, not close enough that she could feel or hear his breath but she had to sense it. Maybe she just didn't care, Josie was laid back like that.

Laid back and unreadable. The most unreadable of all four kids...
Four? No, six. Wait...three have vanished, two still live. Five.
Was it? He could see the bus in the Major Dollar parking lot, see six people standing around it. None were bystanders, you could tell they belonged together.
"You okay, Captain?"
Her voice was calm but there were little spikes---suspicion?
It could be her.
"Yeah."

And then he wasn't on a sailboat, he was in the back of a car or an SUV. Josie was driving; no, the hair was blonde but it was some other woman with a ponytail and dark cap.
I am on the run, the woman is taking me from someplace where I would have been killed.
"And look where I ended up."
Jorge said that softly. Either it was too soft for Josie to hear or she didn't let on.

One of the sails had a slight tear. The three of them brought it down so Cameron could mend it. The desalinator was making a new noise and shook when operating. They had stored thirty gallons---how long would that last three people? Jorge sat in front of the machine and leafed through the manual trying to figure out where he had gone wrong. His mind drifted...

The kids had caught a fish and were covering their naked bodies with blood and offal---

No, they were clothed and the blood was not from a fish.

They are fighting, fighting over the last of the food.

Cameron took a knife to the face. Whomever was wielding it---one of the girls, it seemed---pried an eye out. Cameron screamed and blood sprayed for a moment before settling into an ooze. It was Josie who had plucked the eye out. One of the other girls plunged a knife into Josie's upper chest---

"I smell burning plastic."

Josie. How long had he been daydreaming?

"I'll get it figured out," he said.

"I'm not worried." She smiled, touched his shoulder, and walked off.

Jorge thought of how her face looked when she was stabbed; it was how he imagined her face looked like during an orgasm.

TEN

Cameron seemed to be doing a good job mending the sail. Josie was back at the wheel, moving it slightly from time to time as she studied the horizon.

"You're good at that," Jorge said to the boy.

"My mother taught me how to sew," Cameron said distractedly.

"How long has it been since you talked to her?"

Cameron didn't answer at first; he stopped sewing and looked out at the water.

"She died before we left. Breast cancer."

He shook his head, forced a smile, and went back to work. Jorge imagined the boy next to a hospital bed with a woman dying in it. *She didn't have to die.*

Why had that thought come to him?

Because I understand how cancer can be controlled; not cured but controlled.

"Did you get it working?"

Josie. She had a habit of catching him daydreaming.

"Yeah." A lie; it didn't seem to matter.

And then he imagined Cameron and the woman in the hospital bed walking in a park. She looked healthy, they both looked happy.

ELEVEN

Why do I believe that I know how to control cancer from spreading?
Jorge knew but he didn't; it was something that had drifted off the
edge of his memory like a beautiful boat that slips its mooring. The
three of them ate leftover fish and rice. Everyone had an appetite,
even Jorge who had thought he'd just end up moving his share
around with a fork. The three of them drank a little rum. The
Captain remembered when he had shown the kids his case of rum.
Everyone had laughed and spoke like pirates as they drank liquor. It
was a good night, a memory to be treasured unlike all the troubling
ones. When his glass was empty Jorge retreated to his berth. He lay
in the dark unable to sleep. Josie and Cameron were having a quiet
conversation then the talking stopped. A few minutes later they were
having loud sex. Jorge imagined Josie naked, her eyes closed in
pleasure as she was fucked. He started to masturbate but stopped;
everything felt weird.

When Jorge awoke light was coming through his porthole. The
Captain understood that only one of the kids would be in the main
cabin.
And tomorrow night, they will come for me.
What if he barred the door? Was it the sort of thing that could only
happen at night or would the killer *just strike* at some point,
plunging a knife in his back or slitting his throat? Jorge recalled the
dream of his guts falling from his body and shuddered. He went to
his door and lingered, willing his hand to turn the knob and shove it
open. No one was in the main cabin.
What will be on deck with the blood? Some guts? An arm?
He didn't want to go up there but---
I'm the Captain.
"What a stupid reason," his voice sounded tired. He *was* tired,
wanting it all to be over one way or another.

Josie was sitting on the bow with her back to him. She was watching the sun rise and drinking from the bottle of rum they had shared the night before. Jorge remembered how she had sounded fucking and found himself getting hard---until he spotted an oval of blood with an eyeball in the middle of it. Cameron.

"Sit next to me; it's a beautiful sunrise."

There was no reason not to. Jorge eased down next to her and hung his legs over the side. She handed him the bottle and he drank.

Taking the bottle back, Josie held it up as if studying the glass in the light.

"I think everything is going to be alright, now," she said with a gentle smile.

He looked over at her. For the first time, he noticed a scar above her left breast: It looked like a knife wound.

Part Five:
Memory
is a Place
where we Burn

ONE

How have you been doing, Joe?

And, out of nowhere, an expression of concern or what was supposed to be concern. Joe set the box he had been holding back on the shelf.

"Uh, fine...why do you ask?"

The Area Manager's expression changed---*isn't that the way you look at a crazy person?*

"Every time you walk in the store, you stop to look at the floor just inside the entrance. *Every* time, Joe."

Yep, and that smile--like I'm a Down Syndrome child or something.

"You mean where there is a missing square of carpet?"

Joe looked at the Area Manager meaningfully: *And we both know why there is a missing square of carpet. Why are you giving me grief about being a bit messed up about **that**?*

The Area Manager smiled a hard line smile and looked away.

"Joe...if I may be blunt, you need to move past shit. Your stopping to look at the fucking floor everytime you come to work concerns me and I can't be concerned about my store managers, I've got a lot on my plate."

He looked up at Joe, his face equally red and sweaty. It was hot in the warehouse, not warm but *hot*. Joe understood the dressing down would only end when he bowed his head and promised to change.

"Yeah, sure, sorry I concerned you."

The boss just stared. Those weren't the right words obviously.

"This is real, Joe. This heat, it's why we're out here. The realness...I'm hoping it will snap you out of this shit."

He wiped sweat off his forehead with his right palm and held it up for his underling to see.

"This heat is real, not whatever you think when you stare at the stupid fucking carpet."

"Real, yeah...I get you."

The Area Manager's smile changed; it was supposed to be a *we're buddies* sort of smile but there was too much anger in his eyes to play it off.

"I got to look at my end of the table, you know?" He said.

A lean forward, a "caring" hand on the shoulder, a look of compassion that only made the boss look psychotic.

"Hey--cops have any leads about your lady yet?" The Area Manager asked.

Joe felt every inch of skin, even the tops of his feet, covered with a film of sweat. No wonder people quit the warehouse so often.

Do the cops have any leads? That's a trick question, right?

"It's irrelevant," Joe replied carefully. "I need to stop thinking about that situation and buckle down and keep this store humming."

The Area Manager stopped smiling.

"Joe...you've been through a lot these past weeks. If you need two or three hours just to sort things out..."

"No, no; I'm fine. About looking at the floor....you're right, fixating on it is not a good thing."

The Area Manager looked pleased at that. Did sweating affect the glue holding his toupee on? It *had* to be a toupee.

"Have you checked out that app Larry Listens? I've heard it can be helpful when you need to talk about shit."

"No, but I'm okay," Joe said firmly. "Really."

The Area Manager beamed and clapped Joe on the shoulder.

"You're one of the good ones, buddy, appreciate you."

A wink but sadly no finger gun; that smile and wink really needed a finger gun to complete the package. Joe waited until he heard the back door close before walking up to the relative comfort of the main part of the store.

The girl at the counter looked different---*was* it the same girl that had been there when Dan had taken him into the warehouse? Gina? Was it Gina or Geisha; he was pretty sure her name started with a 'G.' Joe caught himself glancing over in the general direction of

where the floor was missing a square of carpet. It wasn't really a square, technically a rectangle, eighteen inches by thirty---
He caught himself staring and became aware of the cameras all over the store: They were always watching. Major Dollar might let the air conditioner or the walk in coolers fall into disservice but the cameras were state of the art. He flashed a finger gun up at whomever was watching and went off to find the guard.

TWO

The man wouldn't leave, kept pleading with them.

Please...I have nowhere to go.

Thin, somewhere in his fifties, big mustache. Seemed Eastern European. Smelled like mint and cheap soap. Mike stood nearby with the dowel, tapping it into one palm like a thug from a b-movie while glowering at the customer. Joe kept him at bay with a shake of the head. Mustache Man had a few sad items in his basket: A pack of four Triscuits. A two ounce bottle of water. A package of brightly colored streamers meant for a kid's birthday party. The last item was the worst: What did this guy have to celebrate? And, if he had kids, what sort of life did they have?

Please...I have nowhere to go.

Were they one of those families living under a tarp and scrambling for ways to survive the heat? Joe looked up, aware the cameras were watching him and that Dan would be taking note of every minute extra they had to pay Mike.

"Sir, I'm sorry, but you need to leave now," Joe said with a weary smile. "I can ring you up on the way out."

"But, the heat---" The man's mouth opening revealed stained and crooked teeth.

"It's not as bad as this afternoon, I think it's down to 105," Joe said.

"108." Mike, not helping

Mustache Man looked from Joe to the dowel in Mike's hands and understood that he wasn't going to win. He handed his basket to Joe and walked out of the store. It was seven minutes after they were supposed to set the alarms. Dan would note that along with the more serious crime that Mustache Man hadn't bought anything. Joe looked up at the cameras with a shrug.

Once the last customer was out, Joe locked the doors behind him.

"If you ain't buyin', you leavin'!"

Even though his back was to Mike the manager could hear his smile.

"Isn't one in a month enough, Mike?"

The security guard had no response to that.

THREE

Joe didn't need to look at the rectangle of missing carpet to *see* it. No, he saw the piece that was missing---recalled *why* they had cut it out---every few minutes. It appeared in his dreams.

"Bro, I want to get home."

Mike, his Las Vegas Gamblers cap perched sideways on his head. Joe looked at him for a moment and then set the alarm. The two men walked out of the service entrance and the manager locked the door. The Mustache Man was standing on the sidewalk at the bus stop. Was he waiting for a bus or just trying to figure out his next move? *Please...I have nowhere to go.*

The city was full of people trying to figure out their next move, how they were going to make it not through the month but the *week*. A man in what appeared to be decent clothes came down the sidewalk pushing a baby stroller.

"We're all going to die out here!" The man screamed.

Mustache Man didn't like that, he shook his head and walked on. Was there a baby in that stroller? Joe had the feeling there was and that it wasn't alive. It was a quarter past eleven but still 107 degrees, too hot for a little kid---too hot for *him*. He turned away from the man with the stroller and walked down the sidewalk. His apartment was only a block away. Even in the heat of the day it was manageable. How far from work would his new place be? He didn't want to think that far ahead.

Walking Bro was at it again. Did the floor creak like that because Walking Bro was heavy or because the building had been slapped together? Maybe both. His steps had a rhythm like an old rock song playing in the background at a party. It reminded Joe of a get together he had gone to shortly after Jane disappeared: *Come to the party, bro, it will take your mind off that shit.* A stranger, he had started at the edges but after a couple of drinks had been lured closer to the center. Laughter. Hard alcohol. Someone played Oasis' first two albums back to back; Joe had forgotten how great they were.

There had been a blonde in a summer dress. He hadn't really noticed her at first, she was just another soft focus girl, but there were more drinks and she seemed to be flirting with him---
A neighbor started banging on the ceiling; time to move on. Someone knew of a good place down by a lake. Water sounded good, someone had mentioned that even though it was after midnight the temp was still above a hundred. They had grabbed a couple of cases of beer and piled into a crappy old car. The blonde was on Joe's lap. He felt equally guilty and excited...Jane had left *him,* after all. And then what? The next memory was a day or two after the party. He was back at the Major Dollar with a bandage on his hand and a bruise on his face.

Touching his cheek, Joe looked at the unmade boxes leaning against the wall. They were kept from sliding down by Jane's extra wheelchair. He got a beer from the fridge and sat in the chair. There weren't any pictures on the opposite wall but he was fine staring at nothing. Four days. Four days and then he was going---
No idea.
Please...I have nowhere to go.
He drank, the earth spun some more and took the minutes along.

Jane's stuff was already gone: Her parents had sent over some guys with unmade boxes and tape. They hadn't looked like professional movers; professional movers don't usually wear thousand dollar suits and chic sunglasses. None of them had said a word to Joe. Words weren't necessary; he knew who had sent them. Joe had just sat on the bed and watched them work as he drank beer. They had Jane's stuff out in under an hour.
You do not need to file a police report, Joe. I will take care of it.
Jane's father had said that a week before he sent the men in the thousand dollar suits to box up his daughter's stuff. Her dad's suits were a lot more than a thousand dollars and he smelled like coffee and teak. He hadn't taken off his sunglasses during that conversation---had Joe ever seen Mr. Chen's eyes?

173

No...just as he had never learned Mr. Chen's first name--
He was just the *white guy dating his daughter*. If things had gone on longer then maybe some *discouragement* would have been applied.
The can of beer was empty, Joe shook it absent-mindedly.
Not just a white guy but a defective white guy.
He threw the empty can at the opposite wall. The last drops of beer arced and fell in slow motion onto the carpet.

FOUR

After an hour there were three empty beer cans at the base of the opposite wall. Joe hadn't moved from the wheelchair aside from walking to the fridge or to the bathroom to piss. Each time he had studied the bars next to the toilet, one time he had rubbed them gently...

Had he loved her or was telling himself that an excuse to feel sorry for himself?

They had known each other for a year, had certainly said those three words to each other, but---

She was gone.

And he wasn't sure if he really missed her or if he was glad to be alone and have his space again while understanding that he needed to feel sorrow for her absence.

Joe...Mrs. Chen and I have made peace that she was probably abducted and murdered for her organs. You know there is a large black market for such things.

Right, like someone like Mr. Chen would allow something like that to happen. *He* probably ran a ring like the one he had described. Fucker.

She had to love him, right? She had stood by him or at least continued to be his girlfriend during the treatments. That whole situation had started with bizarre dreams: Him and Jane riding in some shitty car through the desert with a couple of other people, ravens circling, demon trucks bearing down on them---

Where *had* they met? The treatments had affected his memory. Right, *the office*. He was a temp and she was a manager. Joe had only quit when they moved in together, company policy or something. Somehow he had landed the store manager position at the Major Dollar.

After the dreams and hallucinations had gone on for a couple of weeks Jane had insisted that he visit her family doctor and not the iffy clinics he had been to in the past. He had demurred, especially when the doctor recommended specialists and tests.

175

I can't afford this, that one doctor…
Relax. Don't worry about money. I got this, you just get better.
And he had smiled and thanked her while inside---
Inside: *She is in lower management in a mid-sized company, how can she afford this?*

The tests revealed a mass on his brain and the specialists recommended that Joe's skull be opened up so they could have a peek. The patient was certain that he was going to die. It was one thing for Jane to pay for the specialists and tests but *brain surgery*? That had to be in the hundreds of thousands. Jane told him that she would handle it, that she had *heard of programs* that would help pay for medical expenses. Programs. Wouldn't signing up for a program and going through waiting lists take years? That thought unvoiced: He was scared and wanted to get whatever was wrong taken care of; if Jane could make that happen so be it. While waiting for his surgery the dreams had continued: Jane was a hired assassin using her wheelchair as a cover. She told him that the dreams were silly but she would look away when she said that or cover her breasts if she was naked.
And there was the gun he had found in her bag---was it a Glock? Joe didn't know guns but it looked like what they called a *Glock* on television shows. He hadn't wanted to touch it, just opened the bag wide enough to get a good look.
There's a gun in your bag.
Yeah, it's a crazy world out there and I can't exactly run away from bad guys.
Had they made love or even fucked after that incident? Joe was pretty sure they hadn't.
The doctors had opened his skull expecting to find the mass on his brain was cancer. No, there was something that looked like a quail egg and inside that mass was a baby tapeworm. After removing it and a couple of rounds of anti-parasite treatments Joe had recovered and the dreams ended. He was healthy again, had landed a job he hadn't expected to land, and had a live-in girlfriend.

Well, two out of three. Jane had disappeared one of the many evenings he worked past midnight.

You do not need to file a police report, Joe. I will take care of it.

That had been a month earlier. Now the lease was ending on the apartment and he had three days to find another place.

FIVE

Joe. the customer is lying by the front door. He's fucking up the carpet.

Gina or Geisha had said that. No---now he was thinking that it had been an 'M' name: Mary or Mara or Mina; an anxious girl with bad skin, maybe nineteen. He had been in the back of the store with a bunch of frightened customers. The police had ordered them back there.

Why did he get all aggro? The sign says everything has to be checked in.

Mara or Mary or whatever her name was had pulled out her phone, started a round of Boomvest, and then looked in the general direction of the entrance doors.

"They'll never get that out of the fucking carpet, they'll have to cut that shit out of it," the girl had said.

"Don't swear in front of the customers," he mumbled.

Kelsey. Her name was Kelsey.

SIX

How much had he slept? A couple of hours? A few? Joe took a long enough shower that the meter in the bathroom started beeping and a robotic voice came out of the speaker mounted above the mirror.
"Ten gallons! Ten gallons! Half of the daily water allotment has been used!"
"Yeah, yeah, fucking yeah."
Pulling the curtain aside he found himself staring at the bars next to the toilet---
He felt *something*, some sort of loss or hurt; that *had* to mean that he loved her, right?
Then..where were all of his remaining memories of Jane in that apartment?
There were no memories of him pushing her through a park or eating in a favorite restaurant or anything like that.
Favorite mutual song? No. Favorite show to binge watch? Again, nothing.
And further back no memories of how it had all started in that office where they supposedly hooked up.
Was her pubic area shaved or not? Again, fucking nothing.
The dreams were still there, though, vivid as fucking always: The two of them in the backseat of a shitty SUV as they drove through what appeared to be Hell.

Having some extra time, Joe brought up the police department website. They had a menu option for following up on a missing person report.
You do not need to file a police report, Joe. I will take care of it.
That meant that Mr. Chen had filed one, right? In any event, you needed to register and set up a password and all that crap. Joe did so.
An avatar came up on his laptop screen; it looked so much like Joe that it made him uneasy.
"How can I help you today?"
So bright, so cheery; maybe it wasn't so much like him after all.

"I want to check on the status of a missing person report."

"Sure thing. Is this a family member or a spouse?

"Spouse." Maybe he could get away with it.

"Sure thing...your spouse's name?"

"Jane Chen."

The avatar just stared at Joe. It was like looking in the mirror again and made it feel like worms were coming to life under his skin.

"There hasn't been a missing report filed for Jane Chen."

"How far back are you checking?"

"One year. I am limited to one year."

"Okay...thanks."

Joe closed the laptop.

You do not need to file a police report, Joe. I will take care of it.

Maybe it was an Asian thing, handling your own shit instead of trusting the authorities.

No, there was something else to it, Joe's instincts wouldn't let that one go.

You don't file a missing person report if the person is not actually missing.

Joe checked the time on the laptop. He was running late.

With no time for food he found some clean clothes and brushed his teeth. On the way out he paused to look at Jane's spare wheelchair. What had been the name of the company they had both worked at? *Why is my memory still fucked? Weren't the treatments supposed to fix that?*

He verified that his keys were in his pocket and opened the front door. One of the "movers" was standing there in a thousand dollar suit and chic sunglasses.

"No," he said firmly.

SEVEN

It was ten o' clock and already 106 degrees. They had been stocking up a bunch of Mother's Day shit---that meant it was late April or early May, right?

How hot would it be by the Fourth of July?

A mess of people were waiting at the bus stop in front of the Major Dollar. One little boy had a majestic bottle of water, at least thirty-two ounces, that made Joe thirsty just looking at it. He saw people stealing glances at the bottle; how long until that poor kid got jacked for his water? A little girl approached the boy with the beautiful bottle of water and told him to hand it over.

You'd better give me that or I'll fucking cut you!

Did she really say that? What was she...eight? Mean girl was rummaging around in her bag. The boy looked scared and looked around for anyone who would protect him; all the so-called grown-ups were making a point to mind their own business.

Really? Is it on me to be the fucking grown up?

Joe walked towards the mean girl but the bus was pulling up in a cloud of diesel and rattles. Everyone lined up and got on and Joe just watched satisfied but not satisfied that it wasn't his problem anymore.

EIGHT

Joe walked into the Major Dollar. He could smell the dying coolers and wondered how many people the spoiling food had made sick. Three steps in the shop the manager stopped to look at the missing square of carpet. Catching himself he glanced up at the camera with a sheepish smile and shake of his head. There hadn't been as much blood as he had expected when the EMTs took the man away. It had been left to Joe to cut away the carpeting and padding with a utility knife.

There had been a flash, down there on his hands and knees:
He was back in that crappy SUV with Jane as she was taping something together---plastic grocery bags?
"You falling asleep at the wheel, chief?"
Dan. Right, he was at the store to drill the employees about what to say if approached by the media: *Here is the card of Major Dollar media relations, please contact them.*
Debrief, that was the work the Regional Manager had used---what a schmuck.
"No---when will the carpet people be here?" Joe had asked.
"Carpet people?" Dan had made the sort of face you make when you catch someone fucking a collie.
"To replace this piece of carpet I'm cutting out."
The Area Manager had winced and then started backing away with a half smile. One hand twitched as if about to form a finger gun.
"Fill out a request for it, I'm sure they'll take care of it. Thanks, Joe, appreciate you."

Mike nodded at his boss and smacked his palm with the three foot dowel.
"Mr. Smith? Hey...Mr. Smith?"
The girl behind the counter needed something. Was it the same girl from yesterday? Nancy? Noelle? No, she looked Hispanic...
Maria, her name was *Maria*.

They hadn't been Mother's Day decorations, they had been *Easter* decorations. That made it---what? Early April? And it was already 106 degrees before noon. How hot had it been the previous April. Again, *memory*...or lack thereof.

Joe busied himself with tasks that kept him within sight of the missing rectangle of carpet, purposefully doing things with his tablet as more of the memory of that afternoon returned. For some reason he wasn't remembering Mike as the security guard. No, it was a tall Black woman with crazy looking eyes. A Black man had walked in carrying something. The girl behind the counter had called out for him to check in his parcel. The customer hadn't liked that, had said he was being hassled because he was Black. The customer had gone from smiling to angry in a flash and---
Joe's tablet was beeping, a message was coming in from Regional: *We see you looking at it.*

NINE

"Someone told me it's supposed to be 116 degrees today; ain't supposed to be 116 in April."

"Whatever."

"Me and my crew thinkin' of going to the beach after work, ocean would be nice right now."

"The beach? Man, that place so crowded you can barely get down to the water so many fools there. Bro told me some kid got drowned by accident, kid was just fucking around in the water and all these people were going in and crowded him into deeper water."

"That fucked up, for reals."

Mike and Maria were talking at the counter. Joe half listened to them as he pretended to check shelves nearby. He had been thirsty since seeing the bus stop kid with that big bottle of water. Major Dollar didn't have a drinking fountain, you had to find a cup somewhere and then scan your badge to make one of the taps work. If you used too much water you got a reprimand, it didn't matter if it was the tap or the toilet. Joe was supposed to reprimand his employees about using water but never felt like it. In the end, he got reprimands for not giving reprimands.

The ocean. That sounded really good. Not just the relatively cool water, something else, something that had been lost when his memory went to shit.

What *had* the black guy been carrying that he hadn't wanted to check in?

Had it been Mike who called the cops? No, Joe kept seeing the black female security guard when he remembered the situation.

Had it been the girl at the counter (what was her name)?

Had it been *him*?

The police had shown up; okay, *that* was coming back. The police had shown up and the yelling customer had been shot. Had he said anything? Had he screamed or moaned or just fell dead and silent? Again, unknown.

184

TEN

The loss of memory was troubling. What if, while digging around in his brain, the doctors had damaged something? What if the memory situation got worse and worse until he couldn't remember who he was or how to wipe his ass or other really basic stuff like that? Joe went back into the warehouse. It was hot back there, mid-nineties at least. The heat was good, it was real, away from the conversations and distorted music and smells of the showroom. He leaned against some boxes and closed his eyes. Even with his weight on them the boxes didn't shift or give. They felt solid and Joe wondered what was inside them. He was in a dark, warm world that was quickly becoming too warm. Joe opened his eyes and checked his phone history for the doctor's number. When he dialed it, the number rang twice and then there was a shrill sound followed by a robotic voice telling him that the number he was calling was invalid. Not temporarily out of service, not changed---*invalid*.

Since when did that happen to doctor's offices? Your doctor's office was supposed to be *bedrock*, something solid, something always there like your parents' house. Joe put his phone away and walked back into the showroom.

ELEVEN

"Store Manager to aisle four, Store Manager to aisle four."
Mike looked like a robot that had been powered down: Hunched over. Expressionless. Batteries low. He was being yelled at by an enormous woman in a scooter with garish red hair: Fire Lady Hair Dye, aisle six. No longer in stock, possibly recalled. Seeing the customer on her scooter brought back Jane and Joe struggled to remember places they'd been besides the apartment. There *had* to be a memory of a restaurant, the two of them looking at each other fondly over a table, big glasses of water next to their plates, condensation rings because the glasses were *full* of ice and that water was *cold*.
"Store Manager to aisle four, Store Manager to aisle four."
Mike's voice was a flat line. He was in hell; they all were.
Joe closed his eyes, desperate for a memory, but nothing was there---
Except Jane in the back of an SUV, handing him a bottle of water, joking that if he threw it up she'd kick his ass.
"Store manager to aisle four, for the love of God."
Joe walked down the aisle and stood at attention next to the lady like he was in boot camp and she was the drill instructor. Mike looked relieved as he backed away, the customer turning her anger on Joe who smiled and nodded from time to time, reciting some words meant to appease.
Come on, there has to be something--did I have something I did like rubbing her shoulders as I pushed her in the chair? Did we get close enough that I'd help her in the shower or getting on and off the toilet? Were either of those things easy or difficult for her?
Again, unknown. Absolutely fucking unknown.

Joe found himself in the bathroom. What had happened to the customer? What had he said to make her go away? It was gone from his mind but that wasn't faulty memory, that was survival. He swiped his badge over the meter for the tap and filled a mug from the showroom. There was no ice and it was lukewarm but it was still water. Joe put some of it on his hands and splashed the sweat off his face.

A stranger was looking back: A Black man. The angry customer.

Is this what I have always looked like? I don't remember...

Joe closed his eyes.

Now you are being ridiculous, you know what you look like.

He opened his eyes and the man in the mirror was again white, somewhere in his late thirties, tired looking.

Soon to be homeless.

TWELVE

A bus that ran all night came within a mile of the sea. It was 104 degrees when Joe set the alarm and locked up the store for the night. He told Mike he'd see him the next day but the guard was already walking off listening to music. Sliding his ID card in his pocket, the manager looked down the street he'd be walking down for overt danger. *Subtle* danger was everywhere, there was nothing you could do about it. Joe could still see the Major Dollar from the bus quece. He had never seen it from that angle; the side away from the street was all cracking cinder blocks and water stains. The manager had heard of buildings made to last a millennium, the Major Dollar clearly wasn't one of them.

The man with the baby carriage was down the road shouting his line. Joe feared him coming along but the bus rolled up before that happened. When it stopped the smoke caught up and encircled the people at the quece. No one seemed to notice. Even at half past eleven the transit was full to capacity, the air conditioning shuddering as it struggled to keep up. Joe found an open seat at the rear and checked with the back of his hand to make sure it was dry. Off to the right, a teenager was playing a rap song for another teenager, describing it as something he'd done that day. It was surprisingly good. The world seemed a hard scraped place, all grit and desperation, but you'd still find art in these odd corners just hanging there like fragments of color.
Golden---she told me my eyes were golden.
A memory, one that felt real. he had to smile at that.
The engine was roaring but the bus wasn't moving. *Transmission,* Joe thought, feeling his mouth change as the smile disappeared. And then a vision of sitting on the side of the freeway in the backseat of a car as another driver cursed and worked a shift lever. "Look, bro, bus people." The teenager stopped playing his song. Joe looked over; an ancient school bus painted a dozen colors was coming around the stalled city transit. Men and women were leaning

out the windows, smiling and waving. They looked so happy Joe found himself smiling again; he wasn't the only one.

"Happy midnight!" One of the bus people called.

"Be free, be happy!" Another of their numbers yelled.

Even the hard looking teenagers looked like kids again, waving to the hippies and laughing. The transmission on the transit caught and the city bus lurched forward.

THIRTEEN

Be free, be happy...
He should have been home, should have been pacing and figuring out where he'd be living in two days time; his conscious mind was reminding him of obligations and expectations, things he needed to do to continue his life---
His unconscious mind was weaving through that, leaving glittering threads like the words of a smiling stranger half unheard.
And the night bus moved through the city, rattling and coughing past apartment complexes and malls and tarp communities. People got and got off, taking and bringing their smells and whatever energy their emotions created.

More details of the Angry Customer were coming back: Protests about checking whatever he had at the counter. The way his pacing had gotten jerkier. Nodding his head, a bitter twist of smile formed and then dissolved. What had he not wanted to check in? Joe could recall the Angry Customer cradling it, but what it was remained unclear. The camera needed to tilt down.
Be free, be happy.
Joe closed his eyes and tried to focus on the Angry Customer and see what was in his arms, but he kept going back to the Bus People. It had to be a hard life, right? Cops bothering you. Scratching and struggling for food and what not. That old bus probably didn't have air conditioning and yet they looked happy like children---
Children who had never hardened and threatened other children at bus stops.
How was that even possible?

"End of the line!"
The Angry Customer had been pacing by the shopping carts. Why hadn't he just left? In his memory, the security guard was Mike again. He had been tapping the dowel on his hand but across the

showroom from the Angry Customer, as far away as he could get and still be able to see the pacing man.

The cops had come, they had yelled at the Angry Customer and he---

Had they shot him because he refused their orders or because he reached under his coat?

Joe could only see him from the chest up for some reason.

Where had he been when the cops shot the Angry Customer?

"Hey, end of the fucking line!"

The transit was empty and the driver had started down the aisle, a taser in one hand and pepper spray in the other. Joe nodded and got up, walking to the nearest door.

"Beach closed at ten," the driver grunted, turning back towards the front of the bus.

Joe said nothing in response. The beach technically closed at ten but there were people out there twenty-four hours a day from March until November, too many of them to remove. The police had contemplated chasing them off, using lethal force if necessary, but then who would have cleared the dead bodies? There wasn't money in the budget for that; Joe had read something along those lines earlier in the year.

He could remember that but he couldn't remember Jane's favorite food or what shampoo she used.

Some people slept on the beach, some just stood in the water up to their hips or their chests or their knees and looked west. There were hundreds of people but it was quiet. On the edge of the parking lot were enormous vending machines now secured behind heavy metal gates. During the day armed guards stood beside them.

Joe knew that but he didn't know if Jane liked to read and if she did what her favorite books were. He took a couple of steps into the sand. The place was so familiar but it was a deja vu familiar and not a placeable memory of having been there. The store manager weaved around the sleeping bodies or the groups or couples engaged in quiet conversation. What would it be like to walk into the water up to his hips or chest or knees? What would it be like to just keep walking until the water was over his head? Would it gradually get deeper and deeper or would it just drop off at some point? What would that be like? Joe sat down in the sand and removed his shoes and socks. He rolled his pant legs up to his knees and walked into the sea. The water was colder than expected and felt oily on his skin. He closed his eyes. Jane waited for him there, in his thoughts, sitting on his lap and moving his hands to her breasts. Joe could smell her shampoo, it smelled like fruit. The manager took another step, the cuffs of his pant legs getting wet.

Where had *he* been when the Angry Customer had been shot? His memory claimed that he had been behind the counter, that the cops had ordered him back there. Yes, that was what had happened; and now he could see what the Angry Customer was holding---a box. A box maybe a foot and a half square neatly wrapped in brown paper. And then the shots. Was the man grimacing in pain? Was he crying out or shouting *You fucking shot me!*? No, he was smiling.

FOURTEEN

Joe walked out of the water and across the beach. His plan had been to sit on a curb to put his shoes and socks back on but it felt good to be barefoot. A garish looking school bus pulled into the parking lot, a short one splattered and brushed and sprayed with several different colors of paint. The windows were open but no one was leaning out to shout and laugh or anything like that.

The front doors opened with a small shriek.

Joe walked onto the parking lot, the asphalt finally cool enough to cross shoeless. He walked past all the faded and breaking cars until he reached the steps into the bus.

Joe set his shoes and socks on the asphalt and climbed inside.

INTERLUDE: THE RAVENS

Three ravens circled. Beneath them was earth dry as talcum and brush they watched for movement. A highway cut through the desert with faded asphalt and the occasional automated truck. A car was parked on the side of the road, an older silver SUV with one back door open. The ravens were circling over it, the circles sometimes dropping like invisible rings closer to the vehicle only to return higher to the sky. Leading away from the dead SUV were depressions, footprints, following the faded asphalt parallel into the distance.

coda:
THe PIer

The keys to the Hyundai made a slight splash. How deep was the water there? Would the keys ever be found? Did anyone ever dive off the edge of the pier---or---what were the odds of a fish snagging the keys at some point?

"I know of a restaurant near here. Good place to get some food, a couple of beers," the driver said, looking at each of her companions in turn.

"Beer sounds good right about now." Jane, touching the railing where someone had carved a heart with initials in it. Joe watched her hand. She caught him staring and looked at him with a smile. They were all smiling, even the driver.

"It feels good being here....after everything." Jorge, hand on the rail, looking out at the sea as if watching for a boat.

"I told you I'd get you here," the driver said. "Come on, let's get inside where there's air conditioning."

She started walking back down the pier; after a couple of seconds, the others followed.

Written 20 May through December 15, 2019

Music listened to: Afghan Whigs, Joy Division, The Fixx
("Beautiful Friction"), Olivia Newton John ("Magic"), Al Stewart
("Year of the Cat"), Thomas Dolby ("One of Our Submarines"),
Oasis ("Slide Away"), Brian Jonestown Massacre (various songs),
America (various songs)

www.ingramcontent.com/pod-product-compliance
Lightning Source LLC
Chambersburg PA
CBHW072236190626
46809CB00018B/2566